The Spirit of the HAINAULT

by

Len Taphouse

Published by New Generation Publishing in 2020

Copyright © Len Taphouse 2020

First Edition

The author asserts the moral right under the Copyright, Designs and Patents Act 1988 to be identified as the author of this work.

All Rights reserved. No part of this publication may be reproduced, stored in a retrieval system or transmitted, in any form or by any means without the prior consent of the author, nor be otherwise circulated in any form of binding or cover other than that in which it is published and without a similar condition being imposed on the subsequent purchaser.

Paperback	ISBN: 978-1-80031-843-4
Hardback	ISBN: 978-1-80031-710-9

www.newgeneration-publishing.com

Also by the same author:

SPIRIT OF THE IROQUOIS

Published by
Pentland Press
ISBN I-85821-314-2

All events and characters in these stories are all fictitious. Any resemblance to events and persons living or dead is purely coincidental.

TWIN SCREW TUG s.s. HAINULT (4367)

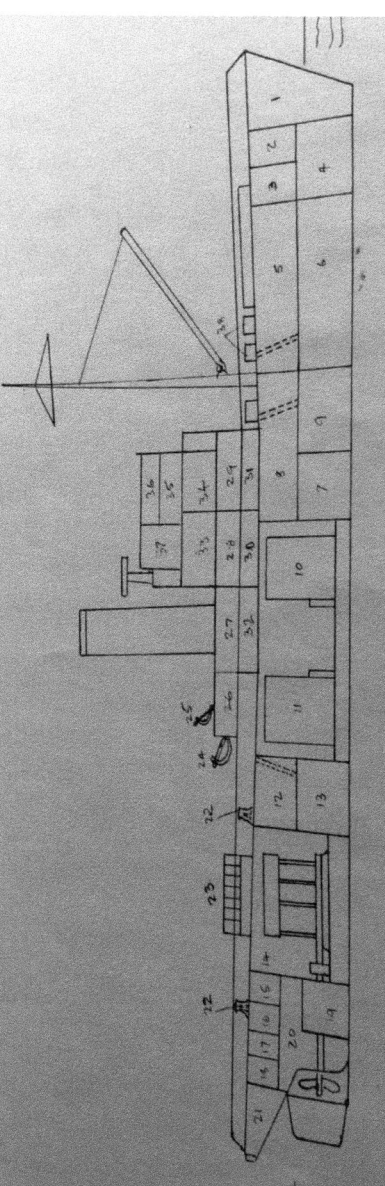

1) Fore peak tank.
2) Chain locker.
3) Carpenter's and Bosun's store.
4) Main ballast tank.
5) Upper hold.
6) Lower hold.
7) Fresh water tank,
8) Carpenter's and rigging store,
9) Cable hold,
10) Forward boiler,
11) After boiler,
12) Salvage pump room,
13) Boiler feed water,
14) Engine room (2-triple expansion engines) 15-18 Accommodation,
19) Engineers stores,
20) After peak tank,
21) Steering flat and Bosun's stores,
22) Capstans,
23) Engine-room skylights,
24) Main towing hook,
25) Auxiliary towing hook,
26-31) Accommodation,
32) Boiler room fans,
33) Captain's cabin,
34) Chart room,
35) Main bridge,
36) Open bridge,
37) Radio shack,
38) Forward winch

Dedicated to my late wife Stella

PREFACE

My fascination with salvage attempts started when I was a young man, when I read about the **FLYING ENTERPRISE**, supposedly loaded with gold bullion, got into difficulties in the Atlantic. She was towed by the tug **TURMOIL** for hundreds of miles through mountainous seas and eventually sunk some 45miles from Falmouth. In 1962 I passed up the River Elbe and noticed the multitude of shipwrecks along the river. Amongst them the Elder Dempster ship **ONDO**, which had grounded months earlier, and I believe, is still there. In 1974 I was working in Tobruk, Libya. In the December, a vessel, the **MERCUR**, was stranded on the rocks in a wadi in similar conditions to those of the **CERCUR**. To my knowledge she still lays there. Derna harbour (Libya) was littered with wrecks, and the coast road between Derna and Tobruk showed several vessels high up on the beach. The eventual disablement of the **BRAER** a few years ago gave me inspiration for the **SANDY WATERS,** and the stories evolved from many other escapades of other ships. I am full of admiration for salvage crews and the conditions that they work under. Though sometimes mercenary, they always work to save lives and the ships.. I make no apologies if I have overstepped the mark in my salvage attempts. Most of the methods are standard procedures. As someone once said to me, "If you can pump the water out of a vessel faster than it can enter the vessel then it will float.

What a pity the **HAINULT**, **STELLA I** and the **STELLA II** were not available to assist in the **BRAER** disaster and more recently the **SEA EMPRESS** at Milford Haven.

My thanks is extended to Wilf Harrison who painted the picture on the front cover, depicting the **HAINULT** towing the **CHIGWELL LODGE.**

About the author

Len Taphouse was born in Upminster, Essex in 1939, moving to Hornchurch eight years later. He served his apprenticeship 1956-61 as an engineer with Harland and Wolff, Royal Group of Docks, where his love of ships developed.

Following his Father's example, he went to sea as a marine engineer with T&J Brocklebank, who at that time operated only steam ships. A year later, disillusioned with life at sea, although still interested in ships themselves, he came ashore and worked as a maintenance engineer with several companies.

He married Stella in 1964 and, encouraged by her, began evening study, working his way up to a lectureship, teaching Computer-Aided-Engineering at an East London College, Although retired from lecturing, and still living in Hornchurch he continued working as an engineer again till he retired at 65.

By this time he had gained another hobby, writing up ships histories. From this he learnt a lot about salvage of ships.

He then took up voluntary work on a steam coaster the **ROBIN** that was built in 1890 moored at Canary Wharf, London. He undertook the overhaul of many of the auxiliary apparatus in the engine-room before embarking on replacing all the deck of the forecastle, a mammoth job. Suffering a heart attack on completion of this work, he took up giving talks to raise money for charities. He still continues with this.

Glossary of terms used

air receiver a storage vessel for compressed air

air start valves   the valves mounted on the top of the cylinder heads of a diesel engine. When starting up, these are opened allowing compressed air to enter and drive, in turn, the cylinders down.

ballast a ship that is without cargo is considered 'light and is therefore difficult to handle.

Sometimes the propeller is not fully submerged. Water is therefore allowed to enter certain spaces to weigh the ship down and make it more manageable

"bends" a condition that divers suffer from, if their ascent from the depths is too fast. Nitrogen enters the bloodstream. Otherwise known as decompression sickness.

bilges spaces usually at the side of the engine-room where seepage, spillage and residues of any liquid substance are allowed to collect.

breaker (electrical) very heavy duty electrical switch.

bridle a Y-shaped cable, usually a steel wire where each end can be fastened to a vessel.

bulkhead upright, wall-like partitions in a vessel usually made from steel.

bulwarks the sides of the ship above deck, about a metre high.

bunkering the taking on of fuel, whether it be coal, heavy oil or diesel oil for firing of boilers or auxiliaries.

camels large, usually cylindrical tanks with heavy duty lugs welded to them, that can be flooded with water and lowered beside a sunken vessel and tied to it. The water is discharged by injecting compressed air, the camel rises, bringing the vessel with it. Some of the larger ones can lift 2500tons.

capstan a pulling machine, usually with its axis vertical, resembling a giant cotton reel. Used for hauling in ropes and cables, usually equipped with a ratchet.

coaming the edges of a hold opening that are raised above deck level. to ensure sea water runs off.

collision bulkhead the foremost bulkhead in a ship, usually forward of No.1 hold or tank, usually made in heavier gauge material in order to prevent rupture in the case of collisions.

double-bottoms tanks that are situated below engines and below holds, usually used for the storage of fuel oil or fresh water for boilers.

dunnage wood of varying sizes used in holds to prevent the movement of cargo.

faired-up reshaped.

fid a pointed spike-like wooden tool that is driven between the strands of a rope or cable to open it up, in order that other strands may be passed through when splicing.

flotsam floating wreckage of a ship or its cargo.

forecastle the raised bow of a ship.

forced draught fans fans that are used to push large volumes of warm air into a boiler to aid combustion and enhance efficiency.

ground tackle anchors and kedges that are laid out away from the pulling area, to give good purchase.

hawse pipe the pipe in the ships bow through which the anchor chain passes.

Lloyd's Open Form (LOF) If a stricken ship accepts an offer of salvage, a binding contract is created. I specifies no particular sum for the salvage job. In the intrests, the reward is usually determined by an arbitration court. The value of the ship, its cargo and freight at risk are taken into account when the arbitrator decides what the award should be, and the extent of the dangers and the difficulty of the salvage.

neap tide exceptionally low tide, occurs once every month providing there are no storms or high winds present.

parbucling a method of lifting a wreck using two vessels with a clever arrangement of cables to stop the vessel tipping scuppers   the openings in the ships side that allow water to drain off the decks.

settling tank   ready use fuel oil tank, usually situated high in the engine-room as a gravity feed.

scuba sets   diving set using a face mask and mouth piece which supplies breathing air supplied by flexible a tube from cylinders carried on back.

shear   violent movement of a vessel sideways due to wave movement.

spring tide   exceptionally high tide, occurs once every month.

tailshaft is the aftermost of shafts and passes through the hull of the ship and has the propeller attached to it on the outside.

'tweendeck   extra levels of decks in holds, allowing different types of cargo to be carried, also stiffens up ship

warping drum   a drum, usually fitted to windlass that allows ropes to be pulled.

winch   a powerful machine, steam or electric, for hauling on ropes or cables.

windlass   a powerful winch for lifting anchors.

Contents

DUFF, TAFFY and ANGEL 1
THE FIRST VOYAGE 10
THE ROSARIA 16
AFTER THE WAR 21
THE HAINULT TOWING COMPANY 24
THE CERCUR 32
CERCUR SALVAGE 42
HOME TO PIRAEUS 51
THE U-BOAT 56
THE PAPA D 61
ADMIRALTY TOW 64
THE CHIGWELL LODGE 69
THE CHEYNEY 75
THE REST OF THE TRIP 82
EL MARDI 88
THE CRANKAY 92
DORIA STAR 94
THE VITTORIA 98
THE OTTO ERNST 102
ZELTO AND ZONDO 107
THE HEINTZ 116
THE RIALTO 122
THE HORNCHURCH 128
THE SANDY WATERS 132
THE CONTINUATION OF THE SANDY WATERS
.... 145
THE FREDRICCSEN 154
THE END OF HAINULT TOWING COMPANY 159

DUFF, TAFFY and ANGEL

DUFF

Michael Duff's favourite pastime was to have his son Peter on his tug with him he really loved the boy. As Peter grew up to be a teenager he began to take even more serious notice of the business of barge towing, and decided that he would follow in his father's footsteps. When he confided his thoughts to his Father, he said, "Peter, all that I have is yours, there is always gold in the bottom of tug. Now that your Mother has gone to the heavens above you are all I have. But if you are going to run a tug, then you have to be guided by others, rather than by me. Learn on a bigger tug, before you go on smaller craft tugs".

Peter was engaged as an apprentice with Green Tugs that were based and always tied up at Woolwich Pier. For four years he changed tugs many times, and most of his time was spent towing vessels on the Thames from as low as the Tilbury approaches to the high reaches of London. On two occasions, he remembered, they had even had to lift Tower Bridge to allow his tug and its charge to meet the upper reaches. After four years he sat for his Coastal/River Masters Certificate. Within the space of a further year he was acting Master of the tug **RENNIE**, an old steam tug of 1914 vintage. On several occasions his tug delivered barges to the mouth of the Barking Creek, where his father's tug would be waiting to take the barges up the River Roding to places like Thamesply at Barking, where he would make sure that they were tied up to so that the great big logs could easily be unloaded. Sometimes his father's tug would venture even farther up river to drop barges loaded with waste paper to Ilford. Sometimes this was hazardous work, as tugs could only negotiate these sections of the River Roding at high tide. Usually the rising tide had to be caught just at the right time. The bridges had to be passed under on the rising tide to ensure a passage back. He never knew how he was given the nickname Duff.

All the memories of Duff's younger days came flooding back as he remembered how on two occasions they were left stranded in the mud near Highbury Wharf at Barking and he had been lowered by his father into the mud so that he could phone his Father's agent. Now he had command of his own tug, the **TANGIE**, and was saving up for the day when he could buy his own craft tug, like his father's, and navigate the narrow waterways and canals of the Thames tributaries.

On one evening that his tug the **TANGIE** was in the King George Dock she was steaming slowly towards the lock to enter into the Thames, when she was hailed by the men on the deck of the steamer **PLANTER**. For some unknown reason the **PLANTER** had her anchor down, and the order had been given to raise it. When this was carried out, the anchor had pierced the under-side of a barge which was alongside. The barge that was partly loaded with sacks of sugar, began to take on water at an alarming rate. Duff conned the **TANGIE** alongside and one of its crew secured a hemp rope from the barge and dropped it over the low hook of the tug, and Duff quickly steamed for the mouth of the lock. Fortune smiled on Duff, as the lock was empty. As soon as he entered the lock the gates were closed behind him. Literally minutes later, the gates in front of him were opened and he steamed out into the Thames. By the time he was round the quay that was outside the docks the after end of the barge was well down. He steered straight for the shore by Harland and Wolff's yard that he knew would be completely exposed at low tide. Casting off the barge, he nosed the bow broadside on, and pushed the barge close to the bank. A long hawser was made fast to the barge and attached to the **TANGIE** so that they could claim salvage. In the cold light of the following day the sacks of sugar were unloaded into another barge. Two days later the barge was patched by welding, and was towed away for permanent repairs. Duff received seventeen pounds salvage money as Master and the rest of the crew received smaller proportions. However the year was 1939 and Duff read the dismal news in February about the rumblings of trouble on the other side of Europe and decided that if things got worse he would volunteer for the Royal Navy.

The rumblings did get worse as Hitler's troops started marching through the Low countries, and Duff knew that shortly he would have to sign up. Talking to his Father, he advised him to sign up immediately, as there was better chances of promotion for the early joiners.

He was measured up, given several exams to work his way through, and on passing the exams was given a medical, declared fit and told to report **to HMS BARRACUDA**, a training barracks near Portsmouth a fortnight later. A fortnight later he said goodbye to the crew of the **TANGIE** and made his way to the barracks. For the next two weeks he had to endure the hardships, and stupidity of 18 year olds who had never had to shoulder any responsibilities, in what the Navy called basic training. After this training he collected his uniform and he joined several others that were either ex-seamen or ex-Merchant Navy Masters, in another section of the barracks. Here they were drilled in navigation, chart-reading, first aid and a lot more about seamanship in general. This training took a further two months, and, after having taken five sets of exams, was ordered to join **HMS AJAX** based at Portsmouth. He was now able to sew on his two stripes of sub lieutenant.

When he saw the **AJAX** he laughed out loud, although it was a tug, it was driven by paddles. She had a very high funnel that had a fluted top, that belched black clouds of smoke. The **AJAX** was a harbour tug and was used to pull in and moor larger vessels like the battleships and aircraft carriers. She did not ride the sea well and was forbidden to enter the Solent. Duff was fascinated to find that she was still a coal-burner, which meant that the Navy was a bit behind the times in modernisation. He was even more fascinated to find such a small vessel had to have two deck officers. To manoeuvre the **AJAX** meant that an officer had to stand on each paddle box to view the vessel being towed. Between the two paddle boxes was the engine-room casing, so neither officer knew what the other was doing. Very quickly they built up a standard system of moves. They were able to put them into practice, but not for long as war broker out at the beginning of September, and Duff was posted to the **4367**, a 487ton ocean going steam tug.

On seeing the **4367**, he admired her sleek lines as she lay low in the water. She looked a war-horse, with her blunt, bluff high bow, newly painted, and what appeared an enormous towing hook just forward of the engine-room casing. The first thing that he wanted to do once on board was to meet his officers. The one that attracted him most was the Chief Engineer, Taffy, a sub lieutenant, like himself, also a Londoner, and quite young man for the job at 22. Taffy was quiet natured, and was prone to making witty, sometime lightly sarcastic, remarks. They were allowed only three days to familiarise themselves with the vessel and to work up as a team. Taffy quietly told him not to worry about the engine-room staff as he'd sort them out. The **4367** carried three deck officers, three engine room officers, two Radio Officers, Bosun, a carpenter, cook/steward and five seamen and four stokers.

The deck officers had cabins directly below the bridge, as did most of the crew. The engineers, stokers and the Bosun had their accommodation forward of the engine-room casing.

The **4367** had been built in 1938 by Rennoldsons, at South Shields, on the Tyne. She was twin-screwed and had two triple expansion engines of $16½"-28½"-47" \times 30"$ stroke, powered by two single-ended coal-fired boilers. The engine was rated at 850 horse-power, which pushed her through the water at a little under twelve knots. Her full displacement was 487 tons, and she was 175' long by 38' beam. She had been built at a cost of £52000

After working-up trials for three days, and evenings spent in shoreside establishments, Duff was amazed to find that Taffy was a teetotaller. "First Chief I've ever seen like that", he said. Their orders were to proceed to Liverpool in company with two other tugs, three destroyers and a minesweeper. En route they were to escort a tanker and a cargo vessel that they were to "collect" from Falmouth. The two-day trip from Falmouth was uneventful and they never even heard the sound of gunfire.

TAFFY

While the time of Thomas Jones drew near to leaving school he came home pleased with himself, and told his Dad that the school had found him a job as an apprentice. His father, an engineer, asked him which company he was going to work for. "Hope Asbestos", was the answer. "Oh no you're not", said his father, "if you want to be an engineer, then you'll go to an engineering firm". Taffy as he was always known, was a bright youngster, who held is father and his opinion in high esteem.

They lived in the back streets of Poplar, and Taffy's Dad knew a lot of fitters who lived locally. While he sat in the pub on Friday evenings he enquired amongst his friends, if they knew of any vacancies for apprentices. The following week one of them told Taffy's father that there was a vacancy at the company that he worked for. He said that if Taffy was to make an application, he would act as a reference. The next day Taffy and his Dad composed a letter to Harland and Wolff, at North Woolwich. Within a week there was a reply, asking Taffy and his Dad to attend the works for an interview on the following Saturday morning. They were ushered into the personnel office where the manager explained what training Taffy would receive during the next five years.

For the next four years Taffy laboured diligently under the guidance of several of the fitters and turners. Thoroughly enjoying himself, he became a respected apprentice. His company was often sought after, out of work hours, as he was witty and good company. The part of his apprenticeship that he enjoyed the most was his fifth year. In this year he worked on a multitude of ships, both afloat and in dry-dock. This gave him the finishing touches to his training. The bits that before he had previously machined, and the pumps and compressors that he had helped to recondition, now found their place on the vessel, and he was able to see the function of each. His favourite pastime was swimming and although he never joined a swimming club he was regarded as a very powerful swimmer.

In those days it was the custom, that soon as an apprentice "finished his time" that he left he company and for at least six months worked for another company. The week that he was due to leave, found him enquiring at the local Labour Exchange about another job. They had no problem in placing him in a small repair year at Blackwall. This company specialised in the repair of small vessels up to a maximum of 500 tons. Most of the vessels that were repaired there were tugs, both craft and harbour tugs. They were drawn up on a slip-way, though the company also had a small dry-dock. After a few months of working there he asked one of the engineers of a tug that they were repairing, how he went about getting a job as a tug engineer. The engineer said, "If you ask the guv'nor, you can start tomorrow, I'm quitting today". The following Monday Taffy joined the **DIXIE** as 3rd Engineer and within a week found that to be a tug engineer was truly his vocation in life. He was so proud of the **DIXIE** that one weekend he invited his parents on board.

As the dark storm clouds of war descended over Europe, he decided that he should do "his bit" for England in Nelson's way, and promptly went to sign up for the Navy. He was declared medically fit, by the doctor, but when his height was measured he was told that he was too short. The minimum height was 5'4", and try as he did he could not make the height. The recruiting officer told him that they were sorry that they just could not take him. "By the way, where did you serve your time?". "Harland and Wolff", Taffy said. "Never mind the height, you're in", was the reply. The next three days were devoted to elementary maths tests and others, followed by two days of trade tests. Having completed these with glowing results, he was sent home to await orders.

He only had to wait two days before being ordered to take the train to Portsmouth to be first kitted out with uniform and deep-sea gear, and then to join the **4367** at present in dry-dock. She was having her bottom scraped, repainted in battleship grey and was having a towing cable removed, that had wrapped itself round one of her propellers.

When he eventually found the **4367** he hardly recognised her as a tug. She was immense, when compared to the tugs that he had previously seen and worked on. Once down in the engine-room he felt completely at home. The engines were somewhat smaller than those of the cargo ships that he had worked on while he was an apprentice, and larger than those he was familiar with on other tugs. The **4367** had two boilers and was indeed a powerful beast. There was a good bit of work to be done before they could come out of dry-dock. There was a lot of speculation amongst the crew as to who the next Master would be. "I don't care who he is" said Taffy, "just as long as he stays out of my engine-room". Days later, Lieutenant Duff joined the ship, and within hours had called all officers to join him the saloon where coffee and sandwiches were served.

ANGEL

Angelucci Favrio was born of Italian parents who lived in North London. Two years after he was born, his mother fell in love with another Italian and hopped it back to Italy. For a year his father struggled to look after him and hold down his job. He found that this was too much and one day took him to the orphanage with all his clothes. He legally signed him over to the orphanage's custody. Angel, as he was known as from then onwards, took a long time to adjust to life without his father. When he grew into a teenager he began to develop an interest in catering and spent quite a lot of his spare time in the orphanage's kitchens. When he left school he was engaged by a local hotel as an under-chef's assistant. The rules of the orphanage were that their charges could still live at the orphanage till they reached the age of eighteen, even though they were earning.

When he reached this age, he, in common with many of the other employees was allowed "to live in" at the hotel. A year or so later found him promoted to Assistant Chef, when the previous one had died. Angel was a great cook and loved to experiment. His greatest delight was in making cakes and icing them, something that he had never been instructed in, and therefore was a natural talent. The hotel where he worked was the first one in London to be bombed, and fortunately that evening he had been at the pictures, and when returning found the hotel razed to the ground.

Feeling downhearted he decided that the next day he would volunteer for the forces and get his own back on Hitler.

Within a month he was ordered to join the **4367** at Portsmouth. What was the **4367**, he wondered? At Portsmouth dock-gates he asked where the **4367** was berthed. When he saw her, he thought that she was a destroyer, and when on board, asked, "Where are the guns, and what's that big hook at the back for?" "That's what we tow with, it is a tug you know," said one of the crew. "Bit big ain't it", said Angel.

When he looked at the galley, he was surprised to find that it was coal-fired, and he had only ever used gas cookers. Why did all the crockery shelves have bars across them, he wanted to know? "If you don't have fiddle fittings, then you lose the lot at the first big wave", said one of the crew. The next thing he had to find out was where to get his supplies. He was fascinated to find that in many cases he was not given what he had ordered. He ordered two packets of cocoa and was given ten packets, and why was he given five bottles of rum when he hadn't even asked for it? Later he was to find that a mixture of cocoa, condensed milk and rum was the best thing for fighting the cold North Atlantic. Days later the Skipper arrived on board, and the general order was that they had to meet at 12:00. Angel was instructed to provide them all with coffee and sandwiches. He had never acquired any skills as a steward and therefore just laid them out on the table that ran the short length of the saloon and left unnoticed.

On leaving Portsmouth they called in at Falmouth to meet up with other vessels before they started on the trip to Liverpool.

As they rounded the Lizard Point they met a heavy swell, and Angel lost a dozen plates, as they were hurled out of their racks. A lesson that he learnt very quickly, was to always fasten the fiddle fittings whatever the weather, never to try and carry more than two plates of soup from the galley to the saloon when there was anything more than a calm sea, as most of the soup went over the side of the plate. Never to leave the port-holes open in any more than calm seas, as sea-water sloshed through and when it went into the boiling fat, you got your arms badly burnt. These were the lessons that he learnt in his first week. What upset him most of all was bunkering. The **4367** was coal-fired, and when bunkering, the coal dust got everywhere. Angel was fastidious about cleanliness, and would wrap damp cloths around the door and frame of the galley in an attempt to prevent the thin film of coal dust permeating the galley space. Nevertheless it found its way into the flour bins, and any bread that he baked was always tinged grey. He draped wet cloths over everything else, and in doing so prevented a lot of it spreading. On arrival in Liverpool he put in a requisition for further stores and was surprised to find that he was supplied with everything he asked for, plus another five bottles of rum. "Why?", he asked. He was rather surprised to find that his request for 100 lamb chops turned up in the form of three lamb carcasses, and that his 100 portions of topside of beef arrived in the form of a fore quarter of beef, and he had no experience as a butcher/cutter but he was quick to learn.

THE FIRST VOYAGE

A convoy was being formed in the lower reaches of the Mersey. At 06.00 one morning a busy little patrol boat collected the Captain of each ship and took them to the Convoy Commodore's ship. this was where the policy was laid down for the execution of the convoy and sailing orders were issued. The convoy was bound for New York and was a very mixed bunch that included cargo vessels, and tankers. They were a league of nations, as some were Dutch, Norwegian, Belgian and a couple of Greek vessels. The convoy of 42 ships was split into seven columns that were to be kept to 700 yards apart. For this voyage they were fortunate that they had five destroyers in attendance, and the **4367** was to act as "tail-end Charlie". Four hours later a destroyer started fussing around each ship with instructions to weigh anchor and make its way out into the bay. This assembly took the best part of another four hours, so that it was early evening before all the vessels were safely over the Mersey bar.

Early one morning, when the sky was clear and the sea calm, just the weather U-boats enjoyed, a loud explosion was heard as a tanker blew up after receiving a hit from a torpedo, only to be followed by two more ships slewing sideways after being hit. The order went out from the Convoy Commodore's ship to scatter convoy, and the **4367** could now attend to the victims. Her orders were never to stop, but to always circle the victim and search for survivors. The **4367** circled the spot where the tanker had blown up, but there amongst the flotsam were only dead bodies. They therefore turned their attention to the other casualties. The first victim was the **TIDEPOOL**, and old tramp steamer that was already well down by the bows. Only one lifeboat had been launched, which only contained ten men. Around it were a few bodies that were feebly attempting to make their way towards the lifeboat. Duff slowly down and willing hands threw ropes over to secure the lifeboat alongside and to haul the men in the water to safety. Fortunately they were all hauled on board and all eyes were fastened on the wreckage as they passed through it, in the hope of finding more living persons. Minutes later they saw the **TIDEPOOL** slip below the waves. Quickly the crew removed the clothing from the survivors and wrapped them in blankets, where they were supplied with hot drinks and a tot of rum. It was then that Angel realised why this liquor had been supplied so freely.

The next victim was already low in the water. She was the **STROMBOURG**, a Belgian motor vessel. As the **4367** moved towards her, they noticed that a large oil slick was beginning to spread from her sides where her fuel tanks had been ruptured, and flames were beginning to lick their way across the surface. As the men were engulfed by the flames they emitted screams that chilled everyone to the bone. Duff had the crew rig nets over the side as he gently eased his vessel through the flames. By the time they were through they only managed to rescue three survivors.

The third victim was the tanker **MONTPELLIER** which although listing to 20 degrees did not look as if it was going to go down. Around the vessel were several men in the water. These were picked up without further ado before coming alongside the lifeboat and taking them on board. By this time one of the destroyers came puffing past throwing up a smoke screen and asked Duff how many survivors he had on board. Within the hour all the survivors were transferred to the destroyer which then sped on its way. Duff had been ordered to attempt a tow of the **MONTPELLIER** to Reykjavik in Iceland where it was hoped she could be patched up.

He was told that another vessel would shortly be arriving to escort them both to Iceland. Two of the tugs crew were put on board the tanker's forecastle and they gradually hauled across the heavy towing cable. This was an arduous task because of the cold. While this was being done, Angel was quietly fishing off the stern of the tug. His idea was to supplement the diet of those on board with something really fresh. He had met with a measure of success, as four medium sized cod lay at his feet and by this time the tug was on its way with the casualty. Then his luck really began to run, as larger one had taken the hook and was really charging about, "Don't pass under the boat", he said, "if the line gets chopped by the propeller I've lost you". He shouted for someone to come and help him hold the line. The nearest was Taffy who had just come up from his watch for a breather. As he approached him, he was just in time to see the line suddenly tug Angel over the side.

Taffy shouted, "Man overboard", and stripped off his duffel coat and shoes and followed him over the side. As he swum towards Angel he was dismayed to see the cook go under. Fortunately Taffy was a very powerful swimmer and dived below the surface. Quickly he located Angel's red jacket and pulled him towards the surface. The **4367** was unable to stop or go astern because the towing cable would have fouled the propeller. An inflatable dinghy was thrown over the side and two of the crew scrambled into it and rowed to the spot where Angel was clinging to Taffy's back. When back on board they were helped out of their clothes and wrapped in blankets. Taffy had other ideas, he led Angel along the top platform, of the engine-room and told him to stay there till he raised "a good sweat". "Only then", he said, "will you have purged the cold from your body". Half an hour later Angel left the engine-room and said to Taffy, "Many thanks for saving me Lieutenant, I shall be forever in your debt". "Don't be daft", said Taffy, "I saved you, but I would have done the same for anyone, and don't call me lieutenant, call me Chief". Poor Angel was near to tears, "But you are the first one who has ever cared for me in my life, really Chiefy". "Forget it", said Taffy, "and don't call me Chiefy".

The tanker was successfully brought into Reykjavik. Plates were welded to the hull over the hole, by an underwater diver and the **4367** pumped her dry, the diver plugging the remaining leaks. A fortnight later found them heading south to join up with another OB (outward bound) convoy still with the **MONTPELIER** in tow. She was towed into Halifax and there went into dry-dock where permanent repairs were carried out.

The **4367** joined HX103, a small convoy, bound for the UK consisting of fourteen cargo ships and four tankers. All went well till they were in a position 140 miles west of Donegal, when two of the ships spotted the tracks of torpedoes. Both ships took evading action by turning towards the tracks. The order to scatter convoy was given from the Commodore's ship and the escorts started rushing around dropping several patterns of depth charges. One of the ships in the third column copped a torpedo and began to list. The order to abandon ship was given and those on board took to the lifeboats. The **4367** stood off for a while, so that the lifeboats could come alongside and were quickly hauled on board. The tug inched forward towards the bows to get a line on board. Two of the crew jumped on to the stricken vessel and started hauling a heavier line to bring across the main towing cable. They shouted across, that the windlass warping drum did not appear to be working, so Duff manoeuvred the tug close to the bows and Taffy jumped and he was left clinging on to the hand-rail, and the crewmen were able to pull him up and over.

Minutes later the warping drum was clanking round and Taffy was leaning over the bows deciding how much cable should be drawn in, when he fell over the bows and into the water. Duff immediately rung down to stop engines, and, as the cable was draped over the stern of the tug, Taffy seized the towing cable. Angel, remembering how Taffy had saved him from a watery grave, started the tugs capstan in an attempt to haul Taffy out of the water. Angel knew that few people survived more than five minutes in the water in those latitudes. As the cable began to come up out of the water it wound itself round the warping drum and little snags on it grabbed at the inside of one of Angel's trouser legs to the extent that it started to pull him towards the capstan. He was screaming loudly by the time he was a foot away from the periphery of the drum. By this time Taffy was out of the water and hanging one the wooden fender that ran around the perimeter of the tug. One of the crew hear Angel's cry as he was drawn inextricably on towards the warping drum. Taffy too, heard the screams and with superhuman strength hurled himself up and over the bulwark. With a further burst of strength he raced across the deck as Angel was lifted over the drum with the full weight of the cable across him. Taffy stamped on the brake and, without shutting off the steam slammed the gear into reverse. At this point Taffy slumped to the deck with exhaustion, and Angel had also passed out with the pain, and lay beside him.

As soon as the clothing the Angel was wearing had been cut away he was laid on a stretcher and taken into the saloon. By this time Taffy had returned to consciousness, and was fast reviving.

Those on the **4367** knew that to break radio silence to bring help would be to invite the U-boats along, and while the U-boat might not be particularly interested in a deep-sea tug as a target, they would not think twice about sinking the tanker, and then machine-gunning the tug. The escort arrived on the scene within the hour and rather than transfer Angel by breeches buoy, they came alongside and many willing hands helped to move Angel on board. Each hour Taffy had Duff hoist flags asking the destroyer how the patient was faring. Within the next few hours another vessel joined them as escort and the destroyer left them and went full speed for Londonderry where Angel was landed.

They were unable to find out any information about Angel till they finally docked the tanker at Greenock where she was discharged prior to going into dry-dock. There they received a telegram saying that Angel had a smashed thigh, crushed testicles and four of his lower ribs broken. They expected him to be in hospital for a month. Taffy asked for compassionate leave to visit him but was refused as neither was related to the other.

They were ordered to sail with a following convoy, and a replacement cook was put on board. Homeward bound the cook was presumed lost overboard, and their arrival in

Liverpool timed with that of Angel being discharged from hospital and fit to resume duties. Duff put in a request for Angel to be re-instated with **4367**, and it was a heartened ship's company that welcomed Angel back on board. Some of the crew had even attempted to bake a cake with an angel decorated on its surface. Taffy, who always enjoyed a bit of cake, ate it but reckoned that whoever had baked it had used baking soda instead of sugar.

After a period of eighteen months it was necessary for the **4367** to go into dry-dock, and the crew were all allowed five-day passes. Taffy and Duff journeyed down to London and at the end of the leave two morose officers rejoined the **4367**. Taffy had taken a taxi in the early hours of the morning to his home only to find that the street in which he had lived was razed to the ground. When he enquired at the local police station he was told that both his parents had been killed in an air raid. They had been in an air raid shelter at the bottom of the garden when it had received a direct hit. Subsequent bombing raids had finished off the rest of the houses in the street.

Duff had fared no better, he let himself into his Father's house, only to find food in the larder going off and several signs that his Father had not been there for some time. He asked the neighbours but there was no information forthcoming. Then he remembered that his Father was a particular friend of the lock-keeper at Barking wharf. On going to see him the following day, the news was broken to him that his Father had been ordered to proceed along the river Thames just east of Canvey Island. In doing this the tug had unfortunately hit a mine that had been dropped overnight. No trace of his Father was found, but some wreckage of the tug was lifted, as the barges that were attached to it were causing a hazard.

THE ROSARIA

On one of the convoys that the **4367** joined at Halifax she acted as "tail end Charlie". During the voyage from Kingston, Jamaica, Via New York they reached the area that was unprotected by long-range allied aircraft and was known as U-boat paradise. Three of the ships were torpedoed, and the order to scatter convoy was given. The **4367** did the rounds collecting survivors, which were later "collected" by one of the escorting destroyers. One of the torpedoed vessels immediately blew up and sank within minutes. Another turned turtle and gradually sank beneath the waves. The third, though very low in the water, stubbornly refused to sink. One of the destroyers came charging through the mist, with orders to either sink the vessel by gunfire if not worth saving, or to instruct the **4367** to tow her to Iceland. The destroyer, which had previously noted the condition of the vessel found that she was not settling lower and advised the **4367** to start towing. The destroyer would act as escort to Reykjavik.

Hours later the vessel was in tow with the **4367**'s Mate and two of the crew acting as a volunteer crew, No problems were encountered in the towing and she was safely delivered to Iceland.

Within hours of leaving Iceland, still in the company of the destroyer (who was cursing herself for acting as a nursemaid to a tug) the destroyer went haring off to the north. She had intercepted a weak German coded signal. Duff decided to keep the **4367** on her course for the UK. This was a responsibility that lay heavily on his shoulders. The **4367** had lost the protection of the destroyer and was at the same time unable to follow here because of her superior speed. Hours later, the **4367** received a message from the destroyer, instructing her to join the destroyer at a given position. The signal that the destroyer had picked up, was in fact from a German supply ship the **ROSARIA**, that had sailed through the Denmark Strait alone heading for the Atlantic, in preparation for refuelling U-boats and pocket battleships. She was a 6000 ton motor vessel, capable of 17 knots. She had tried to run for it on sighting the destroyer, and as the destroyer had closed the range both vessels had opened fire. The destroyer had landed two well aimed shots on the after end of the vessel which had put her engine out of action.

On drawing closer, the destroyer observed the **ROSARIA** lowering her lifeboats and slowly steamed round the stricken vessel. The lifeboats had travelled about two miles from the **ROSARIA** when the destroyer stopped to pick up the lifeboat occupants. At that moment the gun on the forecastle head of the **ROSARIA** opened fire, only to fall short. The destroyer's guns opened up and lucky first shot put the gun out of action and the two remaining gunners were seen to jump overboard and were brought on board the destroyer. Surely thought the destroyer's Captain, there could be no-one left on board the **ROSARIA** now.

Several of the armaments officers from the destroyer went alongside the vessel in an inflatable and boarded her in search of scuttling charges. They were fortunate in finding all six and found that the firing mechanism of each was faulty as each had jammed. This rendered them even more lethal than usual, and each of them were very carefully brought up on deck and dropped over the side. The **4367** was summoned on the radio and five hours later joined the destroyer. Three of the crew managed to bring on the heavy towing cable and four hours later they were on their way with the **ROSARIA** in tow at a crippling speed (or so the destroyer said) of 4 knots.

During the night, the cable parted, and the **4367** stopped and brought in the damaged end, only to find that it had not parted mid-way in its length as was customary, but at the eye that had been placed over the bollard on the **ROSARIA**. At that moment the destroyer made an asdic contact and hared off in pursuit of the U-boat. Twenty minutes later several explosions were heard as the destroyer depth-charged the sub. It later transpired that the sub had tried to flee, only to be followed by the destroyer. She had surfaced, and fired two torpedoes from her stern tubes. One had missed and the other had hit the destroyer mid-ships in the starboard boiler-room putting two of her boilers out of action and killing four men.

The sub had opened fire but the superb gunnery of the destroyer soon knocked out both guns. Two patterns of depth-charges were fired with very shallow settings the sub was seen to heave her bows into the air before sliding into the depths. There were no survivors.

Slowly, as she was now under reduced power, the destroyer steamed back to the **4367** and when she was close, the Captain told Duff that his first duty was to his ship and he would be leaving the **4367** to her own devices while she made her own way home for repairs.

The **4367** came alongside the **ROSARIA** and Duff unlocked the cabinet on the bridge and removed four revolvers. He had never even handled one except at fairs before the war. He and the Bosun and two other crewmen went on board and searched every inch of the ship. In the carpenters workshop underneath the forecastle head, they found two men laying down underneath the bench. They were brought on board the **4367**, and for safe keeping they were locked in the store-room adjoining the after hold.

During the search of the **ROSARIA** it was found that the two forward holds had been converted into tanks, one holding diesel oil and the other heavy fuel oil. Hold No. 3 contained 100mm ammunition and torpedoes, obviously intended for U-boats, and hold No.4 was filled with mines to the level of the tween decks. In the upper holds were bags of mail and crates of food.

The sea by this time was light and it was an easy task to put the new heavy towing cable on board, and within a couple of hours they were on their way again. The following day the wind rose and the seas ran high, to the extent that they were hove to for the best part of twenty hours. The wind continued to blow and they managed a towing speed of about 1 knot. For the next ten hours, both vessels received a battering beyond belief, and all of a sudden the **4367** surged ahead as her cable parted company. What was left was hauled in, while the crew laboured to bring up the previously used cable and laboriously spliced a new eye on it.

Those on board the **ROSARIA**, hooked the heaving line on board, followed by a heavier cable and lastly the main towing cable. As the **4367** began to pay it out, it was found to be severed midway along its length. Fortunately this was noticed before the severed end had gone over the stern. The German prisoners had found a hacksaw in the store-room and had found their way into the after hold and had sawn their way through the main towing cable. One of the Germans said to Duff, "Captain, now you will never be able to tow my ship. It's impossible to join a cable of that size". The Bosun on hearing this remark said "You filthy Kraut, you enjoy the hospitality of this ship, and you treat us like this". "Long live the Fatherland and the Third Reich", was his reply. The Bosun's answer was, "I will beat you yet, I'll splice that wire if it kills me, we'll get that vessel home, and you'll be on bread and water till we get home". Angel had been on his usual forage for food on the **ROSARIA** and had returned with German sausages and few bottles of schnapps. He reckoned that there was little else worth taking except for a few hams.

Still with high seas running, the Bosun and his party set to on the immense task of splicing the main towing cable. First the strands of the two ends had to be unwound and separated. The two halves were drawn together using rope blocks, and then fids and wedges were driven in with 14lb hammers and the strands fed in and hammered down with mallets. For eighteen hours they laboured continuously, taking off only enough time to drink kye (mixture of cocoa and rum) and a couple of sandwiches. Yes, by this time Angel had discovered why they were always supplied adequately with both of these commodities. The Germans, from the time of the discovery of the severed cable had been locked in the hold, in damp, cold and unlit conditions, that they were to endure to the end of the trip. They did mellow a bit, until Angel presented them with a mug of tea and sandwiches. One of them said, "I don't drink tea, bring me coffee". "That ain't coffee you jerrys drink, its made from acorns, drink the tea or go without".

The Bosun and his chum retired, utterly exhausted, not only frozen to the core, but dog tired from the double effort of sustaining the bad weather and from the shear weight of the task in hand. The Chippy and a few other hands managed to get the cable secured on the **ROSARIA** and they were on their way yet again. For the following twelve hours they continued to run into bad weather before the seas began to show signs of calming.

As the last leg of the tow progressed, early one morning they were spotted by a Sunderland flying boat from Coastal Command. By aldis lamp the Sunderland told them that an escort was on its way, and that there were U-boats no more than fifty miles away. Six hours steaming if the sub stayed submerged. The Sunderland flew round them for a further two hours before flying off as they were running short of fuel.

No sooner had it departed than a pair of German Condors appeared, and begun very low bombing runs over the **ROSARIA**. Three time they passed over the vessel. Not one of the bombs scored a hit. Then the Germans turned their attention to the **4367**. Having exhausted their bomb load, they used their machine-guns. She was unable to return fire as she was unarmed, but being highly manoeuvrable she turned to face the bombers on each run. Duff and the helmsman had to be later treated for shell splinter wounds, but the Condors hastily left the scene when another Sunderland arrived. The Sunderland was not well armed but it was thought that the element of surprise scared the Germans away. Before the Sunderland left a destroyer was on the scene, to escort them to Londonderry.

The **ROSARIA** was unloaded and dry-docked at Belfast and two months later commissioned as the **EMPIRE FAREST**.

AFTER THE WAR

The **4367** sailed throughout the war, and was fortunate to come out unscathed, though a few near misses had managed to bend a few of her plates. the officers and crew were demobilised eighteen months after the cessation of hostilities, and they like many others, felt that they were on the scrap-heap of humanity.

The Thames was bustling with activity as companies vied for trade to the far east as well as the Continent of Europe, and ships were coming in daily. Gradually, one by one, tugs known as TID tugs (wartime built tugs) were the first to be released from the Admiralty, and found their way back to "normal life". Deep-sea tugs were not selling well and were being scrapped.

Taffy found a job as soon as he was "demobbed" with the company at Blackwall that repaired the tugs and coasters. What he really wanted to do was to get back to sea in the big tugs. This branch of the Mercantile Marine was not yet in service.

Duff has been fortunate enough to obtain a position as Mate on one of the General Steam Navigation coasters, running down to the Channel Islands for the transport of fruit and tomatoes. He, like Taffy, wanted to get back into the larger tugs, and only took the job as means to an end.

Angel easily secured a job in one of the soup kitchens that were springing up all over London. He hated the job as, to him, it was like working on a production line of food. "No class", was what he said.

It was on one of Duff's runs to Falmouth for the vessels dry-docking that he heard from one of the shoreside fitters about the **4367**. She was laid up in the upper reaches of the River Fal, which at that time was crammed with Admiralty vessels of all sizes. All the vessels were considered to be surplus to requirements and were for sale. Duff enquired about prices and found the "fortune" that he had been accumulating before the war was about half the asking price.

He knew that there were only two men in the world who would be interested in the **4367**, and they were Taffy and Angel. He occasionally met up with Taffy and knew exactly where to find him. Of Angel he knew nothing. He went straight up to London and on to the Blackwall yard where Taffy greeted him with, "Wotcha cock".

"I've seen the **4367**", said Duff excitedly, "and she's up for sale, and I want to buy her. You're well fixed for cash, will you lend it to me". "No mate", said Taffy, "but I'll buy her with you, if I've got enough". They caught the night train down to Falmouth and the following morning found them in touch with a Admiralty agent in charge of the sales, who told them that the smaller tugs were all sold. A few of the motor torpedo boats had already been sold as pleasure craft and a few had found their way as rich mans playthings. "At the moment", said the agent, "there are not many sales of the larger vessels and most are destined for the breakers yards".

Duff and Taffy calculated that if they chucked in their jobs and bought the **4367** they could probably survive for about three months before they would be utterly broke. They decided to offer 80% of the asking price and had to wait an agonising week before Taffy received a reply. Both of them in the meantime had gone back to their jobs. The reply stated that an offer of 85% of the original offer would be accepted. Taffy sent a telegram to Duff via ship-to-shore radio and Duff sent back a simple reply, "Buy". Taffy telephoned the agent to say that they were interested in buying the **4367** but only if she was bunkered and watered for the trip round to the Thames. The agent assured him that this would be put in order, and Taffy told him that he would be arranging a money order transfer the following day. That afternoon Taffy quit his job at the Blackwall yard, took his holiday money and bonuses and cleared up his tools, taxied to Paddington and night train to Falmouth.

Morning found an exhausted Taffy being rowed to the **4367** and gingerly climbing on board. It was three days before Duff was able to join him. Duff had told General

Steam Navigation that he wanted to terminate his employment with them on arrival in London, and he too journeyed down to Falmouth. Duff had a good look round the tug and was amazed to find, that in the short time that she had been laid up, how much rust had accumulated on her.

A passing boat gave Duff a lift ashore where he transferred the balance of the price, and bought some food stores and made arrangements for the bunkering to take place. Hours later a dredger type vessel steamed alongside and deposited three grab-fulls of coal on the deck before departing. Taffy and Duff laboured away, shovelling the coal down the chute to the boiler-room hatch. The following day one boiler was flashed up and when a good pressure had built up, was used to blow down the other boiler and rid it of its water and contaminants. This boiler was refilled the following day and flashed up as well. Now the first one could be emptied and refilled in the same way. The following day found Taffy putting steam through to the main engines and warming them through. As the **4367** had been idle for so long, this operation took hours, as the steam immediately turned to water. For ages the water gushed from the drain cocks as Taffy slowly turned the engines by the hand operated turning gear. Later the turning gears were dis-engaged and a small flow of steam was allowed into the H.P. cylinders. Both were excited as the screws began to turn, and they made their way out of the River Fal, and into the English Channel. They decided that as there were only two on board, they could only sail during the hours of daylight, at reduced speed and using one boiler only as that was as much as Taffy could manage, and tie up for the night wherever they could. He would bank up the fires, shut down the forced draught fans to prevent any further stoking overnight, and maintain a good head of steam. Three days later found them making their way up the Thames where they hoped that they could make a thorough inspection of the vessel.

THE HAINULT TOWING COMPANY

The yard at Blackwall was unable to accommodate the **4367** on her slip-ways, but they were able to hire a small dry-dock at Greenwich and were able to just get in. Taffy said to Duff, "we can afford to pay for the dry-dock and few bits and pieces but we can't afford to pay other people to do the work that we can do ourselves. We'll have to do the lot". For the next few days found them scraping and painting the hull and Taffy repaired one of the outboard valves. He also inspected the propeller and its gland and pronounced them good for a long time to come. The rudder, he reckoned, would last forever.

How grand the hull looked, it fairly glistened with its coats of black paint which covered its battleship grey. Below it the boot-topping was bright red, and Taffy had proudly painted the Roman numerals down the bow. The tug was out of dry-dock at the first opportunity, and they had painted the name **HAINULT** either side of the bow and across the stern. Taffy and Duff laboured from dawn to dusk. The wooden deck, for many years neglected, had its joints opened up and re-caulked, and the steel decking was chipped free of paint and rust before being given lavish coats of paint. The funnel, after a lot of discussion, was painted bright red with a black top. The letters HTC were emblazoned either side of the funnel.

To comply with Board of Trade Regulations, the whole of the anchor chains were withdrawn for testing and annealing, and it was decided that they ought to have the main towing cable tested at the same time. With all this gear removed from the tug she rode high in the water, and Taffy now decided that they could spend some time on engine-room maintenance. There was little that had to be done on the main engine but a couple of the pumps required attention, the main condenser needed a few new tubes and the boilers needed a de-scale. Within a week the anchor chains were back as well as the towing cables, and it took them a further three days just to get them stowed. Another day went past and Taffy had raised a full head of steam before he warmed the engine through.

They were eager to put her through her paces, but they needed a third man to help to cast off and tie up. The foreman at the yard volunteered his services for the weekend, and they were delighted to accept his offer. Everything worked well, and the foreman left them Sunday evening with a good skin-full of Duff's booze, after they had tied up at Woolwich Pier.

The following morning Duff with a heavy hangover was roused by Taffy to the delightful smell of bacon and eggs. Who should be cooking it but Angel, whose first comment was, "It doesn't matter how much you tart the old girl up, I saw you sailing past over the weekend and I asked where you had moored I'd know the **4367** anywhere. Now you are on it, I'm here to stay". "Thank goodness for that", said Taffy, "I can't stand Duff's cooking".

Now that they were a going concern, the were two problems that had to be surmounted, - one securing of work to keep them in business and two, the crewing of the vessel, neither would operate without the other. Duff approached the PLA for work and was told that the **HAINULT** was unsuitable as a docking tug due to her size. Ideal for towing ships along the Thames, but docking would still have to be done by the smaller tugs. They suggested that Duff get in touch with the Thames Pool Authority. Here he met with some success.

Across the river close to Shoeburyness, was a row of anti-submarine piles that had been sunk into the river bed at the beginning of the war, to prevent the incursion of German submarines. This extended from the shores on either side of the river towards the main channel where a gap of only about 200 yards was left. this gap was now restricting the movement of smaller vessels up and down the river. During the war, across this opening was stretched a heavy duty steel net that sank down to the bed of the river. When ships wished to pass along this stretch of river a boom defence vessel would steam across the opening with the net to open the gap.

These concrete piles were to be removed. There was a price to be paid for the removal of each individual pile, and the whole job was not on a fixed period of time. Ideal work in their circumstances. Now that they had three on board, there were no problems about manning the craft, as when the tug had to tie up anywhere, Angel would come to the rescue with the mooring ropes.

An adequate working force, however had to be found. The Shipping Federation was contacted by Duff, to find certificated Officers with deep-sea certificates and experience. Some days elapsed before they found suitable 2nd and 3rd Engineers and Bill Samuels as Mate and a 2nd Mate. Marconi supplied a Radio Operator who was instantly nicknamed Flashy. Finding crew was not so difficult, though only two had previous sea experience and they were fortunate to find two ex-navy stokers. Within a week they had bunkered and taken on provisions to last them for a week and sailed for Shoeburyness.

At low tide they anchored close the main channel and Duff and Taffy both went over the side with scuba sets strapped to their backs and hacksaws in their hands. When they reached the depths they started sawing through the tie-bars between each of the concrete pillars. Originally the tie-bars had been about 2" in diameter but due to the corrosion over the years there was not much more than an inch and a quarter to saw through. There was three tie-bars to each pillar, and the work of cutting through one set meant a labour of about an hour and a half. By this time the tide was rising and cables were attached to the two concrete piles and firmly attached to the capstans. As the tide rose still further the **HAINULT** started leaning slightly as she took the weight of piles. Slowly inch by inch the piles were loosened from the bed of the river. At the height of the tide when they were felt to be loose the derricks fore and aft were rigged and the piles were finally lifted out of the sandy base and laid on the bottom and buoyed and placed. An attempt to winch up another from the depths just using the derrick was unsuccessful.

Several hours later the tie-bars further long were sawn through and the process using the tide was repeated. By this time there was four of the concrete piles lying on the bottom, and it was felt that they should be deposited on the beach. Thames Pool Authority was approached for the loan of a couple of barges to save the constant run ashore. It also meant that the barges when full could be transported to a chosen site. These barges were forthcoming and were moored to one of the piles. Taffy also enquired and received underwater cutting gear, and once on board went down at regular intervals while the tide was receding and cut through the tie-bars close to the piles. Small lines were lowered to him so that as they were cut through they could be brought to the surface, and when they had sufficient of them they could be sold for scrap metal.

For a week they laboured night and day working with the tides, with two teams working on a six-on and six-off basis. At the end of the week they used the derrick to lift each of the piles from the bottom and place them in the barges before they towed the barges containing about 35 of the piles, dropping them off at Grays before travelling on to Woolwich and tying up for a two-day stop-over and rest and re-provisioning. Bunkering, for once, was made easy with the addition of many willing hands. Back to Shoeburyness via Grays to pick up a pair of barges and on to the south side of the defences. Immediately they were in position Taffy was over the side with the hoses snaking after him where he cut through as many tie-rods as the length of the hoses would allow. For the next week they resumed their old shift pattern and returned to Grays with over 40 of the piles, and another two days preparations found them back at the site.

The weeks progressed into months and they found that the nearer they got to each shore, the easier the removal of the piles became as the majority of the piles they found they were able to winch out and therefore did not have to rely on the tide. This meant that instead of bringing two barges they had to bring four to the site. Occasionally several of the crew quit, only to be willingly replaced by others. After five months of the now familiar shift pattern the job was complete.

Duff and Taffy decided that as there was no more work forthcoming, they would try their luck in the salvage of the vessels that still littered the Goodwin Sands. The realised that to try this would mean that they would have to be extremely careful to ensure that they, also, did not become permanent fixtures there. They came across several small vessels and a couple of 2000 tonners, but the condition of them was such that they could only be broken up in position and never salvaged. One of the coasters did, however reveal something that was to their benefit. She had a cargo of cast iron ingots and train lines. At high tide they swung out the derrick, and the railway lines, about 30ft lengths were hauled out and left on the tugs deck.

The derrick lowered a cargo net into the coaster's hold where some of the crew were standing and the ingots were placed in the net and quickly hauled up and lowered into the **HAINULT**'s hold. The tide began to fall as did the level of the water in the hold, exposing even more ingots as it fell. Duff decided that if the **HAINULT** was left high and dry and they worked though the hours of darkness they could nearly empty the hold. Cargo working lights were rigged and the generator was exhausted to atmosphere instead of the condenser, this was essential as the tug was sitting on a sandy bottom, and to draw seawater for cooling the condenser would have drawn sand and muck and would have blocked the condenser tubes and for hours clouds of steam enveloped the vessel. They were able to continue working till the coaster's hold filled to a depth of three feet. Taffy began to think that they had over-done the salvage of the cargo when the **HAINULT** failed to float off when he thought it was high tide. Duff assured him that it was not yet full tide, and when the water level was above the boot-topping they should certainly be afloat. A further hour went by and Taffy look over the side to find the boot-topping was completely covered for her whole length. The **HAINULT**, to Taffy's and Duff's relief floated off when the water reached a point only 2" below the plimsole line. The scrapyard at Grays was able to take the metal from them at a reasonable price, and Duff decided that they might try a bit of further scavenging on the Goodwin Sands.

As they rounded the north east coast of Kent, Flashy intercepted an SOS from a coaster named **CHOIX** that was in difficulties. (He had permanently monitored the distress frequencies). Duff plotted a course for the vessel and within ten minutes they could just, on the horizon, see a vessel that was well ablaze. Even nearer, was another deep-sea tug the French **MOREAUX** running on the parallel course to the **HAINULT.** Duff rung the telegraph with a double ring for absolute maximum revs, and slowly edged ahead of the French tug. Then they noticed that the **MOREAUX** was a motor tug and had also put a spurt on. They wondered what the French engineers had done to get the extra speed. "Taffy", said Duff, "we're in competition with a Frenchie, and we've got to beat it to the **CHOIX**". Taffy swore gently under his breath as he and the 2nd Engineer climbed up into the cramped spaces above the boilers. Removing the bonnets from the top of the safety valves, they gradually gave the screws at the top one full turn. Within minutes the effect was felt and they began to catch up with the **MOREAUX**. Then they saw the **MOREAUX** veer sharply to starboard before straightening up for her run into the **CHOIX**. It was then that Duff noticed why the French tug had veered. In its previous path lay a lifeboat low in the water. As soon as it was spotted Duff did a double ring for stop, and the 2nd Engineer immediately shut off the steam supply. However the tug had been travelling at over 13 knots and continued to run for hundreds of yards before gently lapping the waves. For the next ten minutes great clouds of steam were emitted from the **HAINULT**'s funnel as the safety valves lifted. The 2nd Engineer had been unable to give the stokers warning to slow down on the fuelling of the furnaces.

The lifeboat was rowed across to the **HAINULT** where its occupants were brought on board, and the lifeboat lifted on deck with the derrick. Only one of them was injured and he was the 2nd Engineer who was suffering badly with burns. Flashy contacted the Coast Guard and told them of the plight of the 2nd Engineer. The Coast Guard suggested that the **HAINULT** rendezvous with their cutter off Southend Pier where the injured man could be transferred and taken to the local hospital. The owner of the **CHOIX** was an Englishman, as were most of the crew, and the vessel was registered at Boulogne. He requested to be taken back to a French port preferably Boulogne, and was more than willing to pay the expenses. Duff turned the vessel round after meeting the Coast Guard cutter, and plotted a course for Boulogne. Two hours later they had the unpleasant sight of seeing the **MOREAUX** towing the **CHOIX** towards the French coast. The fire on board her was now beginning to die down. The **CHOIX** owner invited Duff and Taffy to his house for the evening and as they were both exhausted, put up little resistance. The Englishman's home was lavish and in the drawing room, each wall was festooned with paintings, mostly in oil, of coasters. "These are all my vessels, both past and present", he said. "The Frenchman disobeyed the first rule of the sea, he passed my crew and me in the name of greed, to salvage my ship. You stopped to save lives and my crew and we are all now safe. I am indebted to you, sir. Not only do I own ships, but I also act as a shipping agent round the coast of France and Spain as far as Turkey, and I hope to extend to the northern coast of Africa this year. I would be grateful if you would tender for a towing job that I need to have done. I have two small tank landing craft that are at the moment tied up in the river Gironde in western France that need to be taken round to the Marseilles. I'm sure that further work can be arranged to be put your way".

"Many thanks" said Duff, "we'll give you a price tomorrow", and set off for the **HAINULT**. The Englishman accepted their tender the following day and the **HAINULT** sped off for the Thames again.

There were formalities that had to be observed. Many of the crew, although working on the tug, had never been required to sign any Mercantile Articles. It was now necessary as they were effectively going deep-sea, for all be protected by these Articles. On tying up at Woolwich three of the crew quit rather than be away from home for an extended/unknown length of time. The Shipping Federation supplied a 3rd Mate and 4th Engineer as well as a further six crew.

Angel was in his element, ordering what he thought was vast quantities of food. He even ordered like a naval vessel: - two whole lamb carcasses and a fore-quarter of beef. He was again dismayed when they bunkered and he found coal dust in the sugar and flour bins.

The formalities complete, they set off for the river Gironde. They had a rough passage down the English Channel and met fine warm weather as soon as they found their way into the Atlantic. The 3rd Mate enquired when they were to change into whites. (For two years he had sailed in a cargo liner). Duff said, "Don't know about whites, mate, just shorts". The barges were taken in tow and they set off for the long leg to Marseilles, bunkering at Gibraltar.

By the time that they were a day away from Marseilles, they received a radio message, asking them to tow a 900 ton coaster from Marseilles to Istanbul followed by two large barges from Istanbul to Alexandria. Duff agreed to both tows, but requested that bunkering facilities be made available to the **HAINULT** at both ports, as their supplies were getting low. Duff also requested the agent to purchase on their behalf the necessary charts. All their needs were met.

THE CERCUR

The **HAINAULT** was to deliver the barges to Alexandria and a few days before arriving the bunkers were getting low and the crew were subjected to water rationing and had a tendency to get irritable with each other. A two day stopover was enough to fulfil the needs, and by the time bunkering was complete the dust had permeated every nook and cranny. Angel was complaining that the bread that he baked resembled the German black bread. An agent in Athens sent a telegram to say that there was a small coaster that had to be towed from Piraeus to Malta. On the 28th they steamed out of Alexandria and set course for Piraeus. Two days out Flashy hurtled out of the radio shack waving a note pad, it read;

XXX (SOS urgent) FROM MASTER OF CERCUR STOP MEETING HEAVY WEATHER STOP WASHED ASHORE IN HEAVY GALES STOP TUG ASSISTANCE REQUIRED STOP LAT 32.07N LONG 23.5E STOP

This was four hours steaming and while they were travelling in clear sunshine and calm seas they knew that to the south of them it was a totally different story.

The Master of the **CERCUR**, Spiros Gregio had set sail from Piraeus without any charts. He was told that on passing the western tip of Crete to steer a course of 170 degrees. He estimated that in thirty hours he would reach the Libyan coast in the hours of darkness, and when he spotted the lights of Tobruk to turn the ship on a heading of 93 degrees and pass round the headland into Tobruk harbour.

They did sight lights during the night and seeing the lights ahead turned left and ran up on to a rocky ledge. They had in fact run into the Wadi Baacon, which at its mouth was about two miles wide, the visibility was so bad that the Master could see neither side. The lights that Gregio had seen were the lights of the local pumping station and they were only half a mile in front of him when he made the hasty turn. The vessel at the time was loaded with about 3000 sheep. As soon as the **CERCUR** ran on to the ledge Gregio ordered the starboard anchor to be dropped. One of the seamen made the precarious trip along the foredeck to the forecastle and on two occasions was swept off his feet by the waves before he was able to reach the windlass and let go of the anchor. The waves were pounding the ship, and by now some of the hatch cover boards had been swept away by wind and waves. Although the waves did not sweep over the hatch coamings a lot of water, both sea-water and rain was beginning to find its way into No. 1 hold. The vessel by this time was rolling about 20 degrees each side and the shoreline at the time was less than 75 yards away, but it was so strewn with pointed rocks, and the seas so rough that to launch a lifeboat would be to invite disaster. The generator was still running and there was no apparent damage to the ship except the loss of the hatch covers and Gregio decided that it was better if they stayed on the ship, and they would have to wait for a tug to arrive to tow them off when the weather abated.

Duff asked Flashy if there were any other tugs in the vicinity that were answering the call, and he replied that he knew that there were no tugs based in Tobruk and that the ones that were based in Benghazi were only craft tugs, no-one had replied to the SOS. Duff decided that if there were any tugs within the four hours steaming distance, that they had been keeping radio silence, and that he should not transmit till they were within an hours steaming of the stricken vessel. Within the hour the weather had changed dramatically and they met seas with 15 foot waves and heavy swell. The **HAINULT** ploughed through for an hour before Taffy decided that Duff should shut the engine in a bit. "Do you want to wreck the engines, Guv", he asked, "you're gonna shake them to bits?" Reluctantly he allowed Taffy to reduce revs. Flashy came up to the bridge to tell Duff that the **CERCUR** was still sending out her distress signal and still no-one had replied, and that the condition of the vessel remained unchanged. Two hours later Duff instructed Flashy to tell the **CERCUR** that they were close to her and to offer Lloyds Open Form of "no cure no pay".

Gregio the Master radioed back that he had no power to sanction "no cure no pay" as he was unable to get in touch with the owners as he did not know who the owners were and only worked through an agent in Athens. Duff said, "I am prepared to come near to you and take you and your crew off but unless Lloyds Open Form is accepted I will not be attempting at salvaging the ship or her cargo". "Then we will wait for another tug", said Gregio. "The next nearest tugs are tied up in Alexandria", said Duff, "and that is two days sailing". There was radio silence for the next half hour. As they went through the spray the 1st Mate spotted the land mass of the Libyan coast and found the mouth of the wadi. Duff rung down for half ahead and told the Mate to keep an eye on the echo sounder. It was reading steady at 15 fathoms said the Mate. "Let me know when it gets down to 5 fathoms", said Duff. Within minutes they spotted the **CERCUR** and could see her rolling on the rocky shelf with waves sloshing up and on to her deck. They stood off at about 30 yards from her as the echo sounder was reading a bare 5 fathoms. Duff was doubtful if he could bring the **HAINULT** any nearer. "Captain, are you prepared to sign Lloyds Open Form?" said Duff. I am not in a position to accept as I do not know who the owners of the ship are", was the answer. "Captain, I cannot come alongside as I will damage my own vessel, I do not think that there will be enough water under me if I do. I therefore propose to fire a line across to you and we will take you and your crew off the ship". "What about my cargo of sheep", cried Gregio, "there is water in No.1 hold to a depth of one metre and I am sure that some of the sheep have already drowned". "Captain, that's your problem, please have some of you men on the afterdeck ready to take a line". Down went the **HAINULT's** anchors and Duff said to the Mate, "I'm turning her into the wind so that the **HAINULT's** stern is pointing to the **CERCUR**, hold her there as long as you can while we get a line on her, then we'll rig up a breeches buoy". After four attempts those on board the **CERCUR** did manage to keep hold of the line and a heavier line was heaved on board. This was attached to one of the after derricks and the derrick raised slightly. The breeches buoy was rigged and very slowly the men came on board the **HAINULT**.

While this was going on, Flashy rushed up to the bridge to Duff and Said, "Anyone speak Greek, they are still sending out messages". Minutes later Gregio came out on the deck of the **CERCUR** and shouted to them, "My agents have instructed me to accept daily hire". By now all the crew were off the stricken vessel except the Captain, and Duff told the seamen that when the **HAINULT**'s 2nd Engineer and Mate had been transferred to the **CERCUR** that they were to bring in the breeches buoy and the line that they had used and up anchor as soon as the line was recovered. As the anchor was being raised one of the crewmen saw Gregio jumped over the side. "The stupid Greek git", said Taffy as he grabbed a life-jacket and dived over the side with a line around his waist. Up and down the waves he went and when he was near the spot where Gregio had jumped, he tried to dive under. His life-jacket impeded any downward movement, till in the end he shrugged it off and down he went. Within seconds he had brought the inert body of the Captain to the surface. He then found that the life-jacket was some ten yards away and thus out of reach when pulling a prone figure. By this time the anchor was up and Duff was turning the **HAINULT** round to bring the bows to Taffy. "I'm throwing you a line", said someone on the **HAINULT**. Within minutes Taffy and Gregio were hauled on board and Gregio was revived and was sipping whiskey. "I'd rather be drinking ouzo", said Gregio, "thank you for saving me and my men. It doesn't matter what the owners say I will now sign Lloyd's Open Form". "You don't have to now, Captain", said Duff, "the ship is abandoned, and as far as I'm concerned it is now on the open market. It is free to anyone who wants it". Within an hour they had landed

Captain Gregio and his crew at Tobruk harbour with the authorities who were non too pleased at being dumped with twelve men for whom they had to find accommodation.

For the next couple of hours the 2nd Engineer and the Mate inspected the ship. The fore-hold by now had about six feet of water in it and although there were sheep swimming about in the lower hold there were several dead floating in the water. The smell of death was on the ship. In the upper hold of No.1 there were only a few dead sheep. The after hold both upper and lower had fared much better and there were only one or two dead. The engine-room in common with most Greek ships was very dirty, and from the oil stains streaking down the main engine had obviously been poorly maintained. One of the gennys (generators) was still running but when the 2nd looked at the engine thermometer on the circulating water he found that it was reading 145 degrees C, and thought it prudent to shut it down. Before he did this he checked that the air receivers were full. They were. "Thanks for small mercies", was all he said. The bilges were filled with water up to the tank tops and when he took soundings of the fuel tanks he found that there was some 75 tons of diesel oil in the tanks. It was then that he realised why the generator had started to overheat. The water level outside had begun to subside and the suction from the sea was partly exposed and was drawing in vast quantities of air.

By the time they had finished their inspection the **HAINULT** was summoning them with her hooter. "What's the chance of pulling her off?", shouted Duff. "No chance", said the Mate, "there'll only be about three foot of water under her when the weather gets better. She won't float even when she's lightened". "how are the sheep?" said Taffy. "Going bad and turning into mutton", was the corny reply.

When Duff had taken the **HAINULT** to Tobruk he had enquired about the possibility of loaning barges, only to be told that there were only two in Tobruk harbour.

By this time several people had congregated on the shore as the weather was now settling down. It was dry and the wind had died down to a chilly breeze. "How the hell are we going to get all those animals ashore?" said Duff. "Chuck 'em over the side and let 'em swim for it", was Taffy's answer. "But we've got to get them up first", said Duff, "if your second hadn't shut down that genny we could have winched them out". "If he shut it down, then there was a good reason for it, I trust my men", said Taffy.

Taffy said, "We can put the portable genny on board and then winch them out". "What, one by one"? said Duff. "no, I'll get Chippy to knock up a crate or two". Duff decided that the two barges in the harbour were definitely needed. The **HAINULT**'s work-boat was put over the side and the men paddled over to the **CERCUR** making several trips till all available men were on board in an effort to get some of the sheep off. They took some rope tackle to assist them in the lifting.

By the end of the day the Chippy had produced two crates from dunnage and hatch-boards that were capable of lifting about twelve sheep apiece, and Duff was back from Tobruk with the two barges. The portable generator was brought up out of the **HAINULT**'s hold and lowered into the barge using the **HAINULT**'s derrick. This was followed by a drum of heavy duty electric cable. "That's going to be a hard row", said Taffy, "how about a push". The **HAINULT** gently nudged the barge till there was only a foot under her bottom, but the momentum was enough get the bow of the barge within 10 yards of the **CERCUR** and a heaving line thrown to those on board who soon had the barge alongside.

Taffy called for a couple of volunteers to work all night. The generator had to be on board and running by the following morning he said. There was no shortage of volunteers so Taffy picked the 3rd Engineer and the 3rd Mate and the other crew members went back to the **HAINULT** for the night. While they had been on the **CERCUR** that day they had been lifting sheep out of the upper hold simply by using pulleys and slings slung round the bodies of the sheep. Some of the sheep had even been slung over men's shoulders as they climbed the vertical steps, but the sheep unused to human contact had wriggled so fiercely that two of the crew had lost their footing and plunged down to the tween decks. One finished up with a dislocated collar bone while the other had strained a ligament in his foot. Using these crude methods they had manage to remove 200 sheep from the upper hold.

Taffy and the 3rd Engineer were on the deck of the **CERCUR** hauling up a heavy duty electric cable from the barge, while the 3rd Mate made sure that it was paid out. When there was sufficient on deck Taffy started pulling the end through the accommodation and down into the engine-room where he made the necessary connections to the distribution board, taking care to remove all other generator connections. When these were made he went down into the barge and the 3rd Engineer hacksawed through the cable and then attached it to the generator. The 3rd engineer and the 3rd Mate both held on to the long starting handle of the generator while Taffy used the valve lifter. "Start swinging now", said Taffy. Three revolutions later he let go of the valve lifter and the genny spluttered into life. "that's my beauty, now we can have a cuppa tea". The 3rd Mate said, "Is that all you ginger beers think of?" "When you get to Chiefy's age, maybe", said the 3rd Engineer, "at my age I go for other forms of enjoyment". After a cuppa and a smoke they worked their way through the accommodation to the after deck. "Let's see if these winches work", said Taffy. There were no problems there and the derrick was raised and swung outboard and the derrick cable lowered down into the barge. The portable generator although large was purpose made and had a single lifting eye above it. It was easy to hook up and very slowly the generator was raised above deck level and brought on board. Taffy decided it was better to site the genny as near as possible to the accommodation to keep it out of the way. "Right", said Taffy, "we've got one more job that we have to do. That genny won't run on air, and I don't see why we should have to use our own oil when we can use theirs". Down into the engine-room he went with the 3rd Engineer to find the settling tanks high up in the engine-room almost dry. This meant that the fuel oil pump had to be put into operation to pump up the settling tanks. At this point Taffy was not sure whether the fuel oil was contaminated with water caused by damage to the ship. As the starboard settling tank began to fill, he ran it down to a centrifugal oil purifier, from here he pumped it up to the port settling tank. When this was full he broke a union at the bottom of the tank and placed a 5 gallon oil drum underneath where the precious liquid was allowed to fill. It was immediately replaced with another, and the first one was taken up on deck where it was emptied into the generator fuel tank. By the time the **HAINULT**'s crew had breakfasted and had come on board they were nearing exhaustion. "Here you are Chiefy", said one of the crew, "compliments of Angel", pressing a bacon sandwich and a thermos flask of tea into his hand. "Bacon", said Taffy, "where did Angel get bacon?" "He reckoned that the Greeks didn't have any more need for it", said one. Refreshed they continued to refill the settling tank to its limit. "That's it, said Taffy, "I'll crucify anyone who disturbs my sleep now", and back they went to the **HAINULT**.

The derricks were rigged over both holds and the second barge was warped alongside the fore hold. This meant that both holds could be worked at the same time. The animals were herded into the cages, hoisted to deck level and then outboard and down into the barges. By 14.00. both barges were so crammed that the cages could no longer be lowered into them. The barges were cast adrift and the **HAINULT** towed them round to Tobruk. In the meantime some of the animals were brought up on the deck and dropped over the side. Only one or two failed to find their way to the shore. Then the second Engineer had a brain-wave. Why put the sheep in barges? Why not build a tower and run the sheep in the cages to shore like a giant breeches buoy? It would save the trip round the mainland and would certainly be easy to unload. Duff brought the **HAINULT** back to the wadi, and by this time it was dark. The idea was discussed at length and approved and Chippy was to start work at first light with whatever help he required. The following morning they found that a lot of the sheep had died during the night, and the men working in the holds had to cover their noses and mouths with pieces of cloth in an attempt to eliminate the stench of dead animals. Two more barge loads were delivered to Tobruk and by that time the upper holds were both clear. Chippy had built a rough tower on shore and stakes were hammered into the rock to guy it. Cables were run out from the tops of the derricks to the top of the tower, and all was ready for the next days work.

The following morning found most of the sheep in the forward lower hold were dead, and those that were alive were quickly lifted out and put ashore. By this time there was a line of lorries and trucks waiting to whisk them away to town. Clearing the lower after hold started in the afternoon, and it was considered expedient to continue working till the hold was completely clear of live animals, and this was achieved by midnight. During the day Duff and Taffy had donned scuba gear and had swum round to the under-side of the **CERCUR** to see what damage was visible. They both noted that the vessel was luckily on a rocky shelf for its whole length and that the hull was dented below the bilge keel. There did not appear to be any further damage but they were unable to see the under-side. They also noted that the sea bottom fell rapidly away from the vessel to about five fathoms.

On getting back to the **HAINULT** a lot of discussion took place. They both felt that the first priority was to empty the holds of the dead animals. Taffy decided that rather than put salvage pumps on board he would use the ship's bilge pump to empty the forward hold. Arrangements were made with a local builder to dig a large trench with a bulldozer further along the beach. The dead animals were to be put into the trench and precious fuel oil used to ignite the carcasses. The bilge pump was started up and the water level started dropping, but the conditions down in the hold were terrible. The cage was lowered into the hold on top of dead bodies and the carcasses were thrown into the cage to be hauled up and ashore. The lorries that had been used to convey the live sheep to town were now used as a transport to the funeral pyre. The stench was so great that the men working down there worked in hourly shifts. Although the bilge pump was running it was failing to lower the level of the water and was obviously choked at its suction end, so it was changed over to pump what water there was in the after hold. While this was being done Taffy and the 2nd Engineer donned scuba gear and went down into the fore-hold to clear the obstruction. Needless to say there was a dead sheep over the suction which they removed. While they were down there they moved several of the nearby bodies into the cage and then came upon deck. "We are going to have to do that a few more times, I'll be bound", said Taffy. The removal of the animals continued, and the bilge pump which had by now emptied the after hold was put back pumping the fore hold. It seemed that the pump would only run for an hour before the suction had to be cleared again. By nightfall the water level was down to three feet, and Taffy decided to suspend pumping. In the morning, four men wearing scuba gear (they only had four sets) went down into the hold to what they hoped would be the last days discharge and then pump dry. However they were only able to work for three hours before their air cylinders ran out. This means a delay of two hours before the cylinders could be replenished, and it was not till midday of the following day that the hold was cleared and the hold pumped dry. Taffy had arranged for several 40 gallon oil drums to be filled from the **CERCUR**'s tanks and brought ashore. These were taken to the trench where the oil was run out into the trench and set alight Those on board the **HAINULT** had the dubious pleasure of having roast lamb dished up by Angel for many days to come, however they quickly lost their appetite. "I couldn't miss the opportunity of a nice bit of fresh meat", said Angel. Even when he dished up a "curry for a change", the moans were, "I suppose its lamb curry".

CERCUR SALVAGE

More discussion took place between Duff and Taffy on how to salvage the vessel. they had already covered their running costs by the salvage of the sheep. "She's not taking in much water", said Taffy, "and even if we empty her tanks, its not going to be enough to make her float". Duff said, "And if we try and drag her off we'll rip her bottom out, as smooth as the rock is". They then hit on the idea of blasting away some of the rocky shelf close to, and under the ships bottom. Flashy radioed an agent in Benghazi to obtain explosive for underwater charges. Hours later a message came back that he had located suitable explosives. "If we don't use enough it will just be wasted. If we use too much, we'll blast the rock away OK, but we'll put a few holes in her bottom as well. The rocky face was inspected and was found to be well pocketed and the need for drilling of holes for the explosive unnecessary. Although they buried small charges, when the detonators were operated the wall of water that rose up resembled that of several depth-charges. The **HAINULT** had stood off at about 100 yards, and once the water had settled drew in closer and dropped anchor. Immediately Duff was over the side complete with scuba gear to inspect the result of the blasting. No sooner was he in the water, than Angel jumped down into the inflatable dinghy and did a slow circuit between the two vessels, and climbed back on board the **HAINULT** with a large bag and went straight to the galley. For some time the diet of lamb was intermingled with that of a variety of fish and squid. "I've got to look after my boys stomachs", was his only comment. Duff's inspection of the blasting revealed that the sandstone slope leading up to the shelf had disappeared, and it exposed a wall that was near vertical but contained few pockets. Taffy grimaced and said, "that means we are going to have to drill a set of staggered holes in the newly formed cliff". A mobile compressor was brought up from the **HAINULT's** hold and placed on board the work-boat. That afternoon the 2nd Mate and the 3rd Engineer donned the scuba sets and started drilling holes in the cliff. The rock was soft for drilling and by the time their air had run out they had drilled holes for half the vessels length. The drilling of holes and the laying of the charges continued throughout the next morning, and by late afternoon the **HAINULT** drew off again while the charges were fired. Those on the bridge of the **HAINULT** were intent on watching the masts of the **CERCUR** to see if there was any movement of the vessel. There was none.

The following morning Taffy and Duff donned the scuba gear to see the latest results. They were somewhat disappointed to find that although the holes had been drilled to a depth of three feet, the charges had only blasted away about four feet of the rock face. "Looks like we are going to have to have another two sets of drillings", said Taffy. The under-side of the vessel was pock-marked with small indentations about four of five inches deep but Taffy was unsure as to whether these were caused by the blasting or the vessel grounding. The next three days were spent in drilling further holes and blasting and they had had to order further explosives. Inspection on the fourth day revealed that the sandstone had been cleared along one side to a distance of about fifteen feet for the whole length of the vessel. Now Taffy and his engineers had to clear all tanks. All the diesel oil left in the ship was transferred into 40 gallon oil drums and brought over in the work-boat to the **HAINULT** and pumped into her tanks. Taffy pumped dry all the water tanks on the starboard side and pumped sea water into the fuel tanks and fresh-water tanks on the port side. "Pump 'em till they overflow", said Taffy, "we've got to get as much weight into the port side as possible, so that we can tip her".

Taffy put power on to the windlass and fully weighed the starboard anchor, then he brought up the port anchor to just above the water while some of the crew shackled a cable to the anchor. The other end was attached to the aft capstan on the **HAINULT** and was gradually warped near to the stern. The **HAINULT** was still anchored, and, using her windlass to pull her through the water she slowly edged along the wadi. At the same time the **CERCUR**'s anchor cable was being paid out, and when the tug had recovered all her cable she used her engines to pull the **CERCUR**'s anchor still further along the wadi. When she was finally a distance of about 100 yards from the **CERCUR** she dropped the anchor knowing full well that the distance would give the **CERCUR**'s anchor good purchase.

After four days of anxious waiting, Good lady fortune began smiling on them. The following day the clouds were in again and the wind began to blow from the north-east, though gently at first. Duff said, as the sea began to rise, "it's today or never. The Mediterranean has no tide to speak of and the only thing that makes the sea rise is the wind, so let's get cracking".

The **HAINULT** steamed about 200 yards away from the **CERCUR** and dropped both her anchors. The water depth at that point was about 10-12 fathoms. She went astern till all her anchor cable was paid out. The inflatable dinghy was used to ferry a messenger line from the stern of the **CERCUR** to the tug and this was followed by the towing wire. This short trip in the inflatable dinghy was a perilous one as the sea by this time was getting high. The cable was made fast on the **HAINULT's** towing hook, and the end on board the **CERCUR** was given three turns round the warping drum on the poop. The cable between the two vessels was brought up tight. The Chippy was up in the bows ready to operate the windlass while Taffy was in the engine-room, and the Bosun on the bows of the **HAINULT**. Duff and Taffy kept asking each other how long they could afford to wait before the big pull. How long could they wait and rely on the sea being high? "Give it an hour, and then let's pull what may", said Duff. This is where Angel came into his own domain, almost immediately a meal appeared. "Huh, fish again", said Taffy. "Chiefy", said Angel, "if that ship comes off today, I will give you a special treat tomorrow". "Don't call me Chiefy", Taffy said sarcastically. The wind by that time had risen to gale force and the sea was running very high. During the time that they had been eating the **HAINULT** had been steaming gently to maintain steerage and prevent dragging her anchors. When Duff reached the bridge he fired a flare into the sky. This was the signal for pulling to start on all purchase points.

The Chippy in the bows of the **CERCUR** began hauling in on the port anchor and while the Bosun on the **HAINULT** gently started hauling on the **HAINULT**'s anchor while she steamed forward. The towing wire hummed and shook itself free of water. Just at the point where Duff though that the wire would part there was a flare fired from the bows of the **CERCUR**. This meant that the Chippy had recovery on the anchor cable and that the bows were beginning to come off the rocky shelf, and that Duff could steam at full power. How the vessel creaked and groaned.

The bow gradually slid off and very slowly she swung round till she was in line with her anchor. This now meant that she was lying at an angle of 45 degrees with the shore. She really needed an angle of 110 degrees before she could travel along the wadi. The Chippy kept the tension on the anchor to prevent the gale blowing her back towards the shore. Duff kept the pull on the **CERCUR** but she refused to budge. In frustration he shouted down the voice-pipe to Taffy, "Can't you get that engine to pull any harder?". "The poor old bugger is shaking herself to bits as it is", was the terse reply. The towing wire was released from the capstan of the **CERCUR** and brought back on board the **HAINULT**. She then moved stern-first towards the bow of the **CERCUR** and a heaving line was put on board and the towing wire was slowly brought up to the warping drum of the windlass. Meanwhile the 2nd Engineer went down into the engine-room and started flooding the forward hold. The hauling up of the cable making fast took a further two hours and in this time the wind had begun to die down. They all knew that within a few hours the level of the sea would also begin to drop.

The **HAINULT** anchored again and up went the flare again.

The bows of the **CERCUR** began to turn still further as the **HAINULT** hauled away and Chippy weighed anchor completely so that she was free of the land. With an almighty groan the ship came off its resting place. The bows slid deep but came up, and there she was, afloat! A cheer from all was heard, except the Chippy who had been thrown on his back by the fierce movement. The **CERCUR** was bobbing about with a list of about 10 degrees and was definitely down by the bows. Duff brought her out into the middle of the wadi and the **CERCUR** dropped anchor, and the **HAINULT** tied up alongside. By this time the wind had dropped and the sea was beginning to calm and nightfall was approaching. "One more thing to do", said Taffy, "I want to take soundings all round, to see if she's making any water". That evening there was lots of discussion, should they tow the **CERCUR** or sail her under her own power.

The following morning Taffy climbed on board took soundings and reported that she had not made any water.

The ballast pump was put into operation to empty the forward hold, but the port settling tank could not be pumped to sea, so the unions were disconnected and the water was allowed to run down to the bottom of the engine-room into the bilges where it was then pumped overboard. Taffy was a bit disappointed to find a small oil-slick spreading around the ship, but just muttered, "Let's be thankful that it's only small". The freshwater tank that had been flooded with seawater was emptied overboard. The small after-peak tank still contained fresh-water, but Taffy was dubious about its quality and decided to dump it as well.

By this time the **CERCUR** had a draught of 6'6" forward and 8'aft and was on an even keel. The following morning they started transferring diesel oil back to the **CERCUR**. It was brought back in the 40 gallon oil drums and tipped back into the tanks by means of a large funnel placed in the top of the over-flow pipes. By this time the bunkers of the **HAINULT** were getting low and she set off for Tobruk to replenish her bunkers and water tanks, and fill some of her tanks with diesel oil. While she was away the

2nd Engineer was running it down to the purifier and pumping it up again to both of the settling tanks. None of **the HAINULT's** engineers trusted Greek engineers, so each of the fuel injectors on the port generator were removed, cleaned and reassembled. The oil lines were cracked and bled of the accumulation of air.

The air reservoir had lost a bit of pressure, but they reckoned there was sufficient to attempt one start. Fuel on, the 2nd Engineer used the hand-operated pump to ensure that the lubricating oil circulated round the engine before an attempt was made to start, air on, and the engine turned over about three times and burst into life. The 2nd Engineer went up and shut down the portable generator, and disconnected the cables attaching it to the distribution board. He then connected up the cables that led to the generator that was running, and with a certain amount of trepidation he engaged the main breaker with the board. After engaging knife switches, etc., the lights in the engine-room came on for the first time. How much easier it was for them to work now. Now that the generator was on the board the circulating water pump was put into operation. Now, hopefully the generator would not over-heat. Next of importance was to put the compressor into operation so that the air cylinders could be pumped up prior to starting the other generator. While the compressor was running, they went over the fuel injectors in the same way and bled the fuel lines.

By this time the **HAINULT** was back with her tanks full of diesel oil and her fresh-water tanks replenished. "Acting as a bloody tanker now", said Taffy. The **HAINULT** used her pumps to bunker the **CERCUR**, and while this was being done the 2nd Engineer started the starboard generator. After running it for an hour he decided that all was well and shut it down for the night. When everyone was back on board the **HAINULT** they feasted on specials that Angel had produced. He had been ashore in Tobruk and had bought a forequarter of beef, and they were treated to roast beef. Also on the menu was crab-meat. "Where the hell did you get that, Angel?" they all wanted to know. "I took a walk along the beach while you fellows were working so hard, and amongst the rocks I found the crabs". When the meal was over Taffy said, "I'm never changing Ship unless Angel comes with me". There was then a big cheer as Angel brought in a large square cake and on its surface Angel had carefully iced the shape of the **CERCUR** with 25% ?? in the middle. "I kept my promise", said he.

The following morning the port anchor was pulled up to retrieve the cable that had been used to lay it out as ground tackle and when it was back on the deck of the **HAINULT** it was coiled and stowed away in the hold. That morning Angel had given them yet another treat when he dished up bacon and eggs for breakfast. "Where did you get it", they wanted to know. "I bought the eggs ashore", he said. "We guessed that", said the crew, "but where did you get the bacon, you didn't buy that ashore, its forbidden in this country". "The Greeks aren't here, so they wouldn't need it on the **CERCUR** would they?"

The mobile generator was lifted up off the deck and swung outboard and down into the **HAINULT**'s hold and the **CERCUR**'s deck was generally cleared.

Throughout the salvage operation, Duff had been in constant contact with agents in Athens, who were trying to trace the owners of the **CERCUR**, but they were an elusive lot. They were finally traced through several holding companies. No wonder Gregio had had so many problems. However by a bit of luck the agents traced the owners as being the Papadolus Brothers, based in Piraeus, and negotiations were about to start.

When the port anchor was pulled up to retrieve the cable Taffy had been in the engine-room of the **HAINULT** and he felt sure that he had heard what he described as a loud clang resounding through the hull just as he reckoned that it was leaving the sea bed. He passed his comments on the Duff, who just shrugged his shoulders.

The following day was spent running up the starboard generator and putting it on the board and preparing the main engine for trials. Taffy was very much a steam engineer who regarded small diesel engines such as the portable generator as being OK but large ones, he loathed, and felt that they were evil, smelly noisy things that only produced any power when they were running fast. Fortunately the 3rd Engineer had sailed deep-sea in a few cargo vessels before quitting to go into tugs, so he had experience of larger engines. It was he that was able to guide the other engineers as to the preparations needed to start the main engine. The main circulating pump and the main lubricating oil pumps were started up. Rather than take any chances the fuel injector units and each of the air-start vales were stripped, cleaned and reassembled. While this was being carried out the main engine was being turned over very slowly by means of the turning gear.

Several hours later, with the turning gear disengaged the main engine, to all intents and purposes appeared ready to start. The starting air and the scavenge pumps were put into operation and the 3rd Engineer took up the controls. He pushed the level to air start and on to fuel, the engine coughed and turned over 3 or 4 times before coming to rest. Now the air cylinder had to be pumped up again. This took about an hour and half before they were ready to make a further attempt. In the meantime the turning gear had been engaged to make sure that the engine kept turning. The second attempt proved no better than the first and Taffy was beginning to doubt the 3rd's ability. However, good naturedly he said nothing. On the third attempt some of the cylinders spluttered into life and the engine vibrated a lot at first until the other cylinders caught and she started thumping over steadily. They ran it long enough to charge its own cylinder of starting air before shutting down.

Duff then radioed Athens to inform the agents that they were in a position ready to sail. The agent said that the owners were willing to give a reasonable price on surveying the **CERCUR** in dry-dock in Piraeus. There followed a lot of radio traffic between Duff and the owners representative, as Duff was trying to extract a price or percentage from them, but they declined to suggest a figure. Duff closed the discussion with an estimate of the sailing time of sixty hours. He went in search of Taffy to sort out the arrangements for crewing the **CERCUR** on its homeward trip but he was nowhere to be found. It seemed no-one had seen him for the last hour and a half. Then Angel said that he had last seen Taffy in his "space-mans suit". Duff began to worry, and quickly donned scuba gear and over the side he went. He swam the full length of the **CERCUR** looking at the lightly dented bottom surface before he spotted Taffy who was on his way up. When they both climbed back on board, Duff tore him off a strip and said, "You've broken the rules, mister. Divers always dive in pairs. You never go down there without telling anyone you were going. Why didn't you?"

"Look mister", said Taffy, "down there is a U-boat sitting on the bottom, undamaged, just waiting to be brought to the surface." "What made you go down to look?" said Duff, "You didn't just go to look at the bottom of the **CERCUR** and just happen to look down and see it did you?" "I told you I heard a clang when the anchor came up. I wanted to find out what it clanged against", said Taffy, "Now do you want a look?" Neither of them could get the scuba sets on fast enough, and down into the depths they descended. In about sixty feet of water there she lay. For a machine of war she looked beautiful. As Taffy had said undamaged, on an even keel and in what appeared pristine condition. When they got back on board the **HAINULT** they had a hasty discussion about the U-boat. They both agreed to deliver the **CERCUR** first and then come back and attempt a salvage of the U-boat.

HOME TO PIRAEUS

It was agreed that the **CERCUR** would make her way to Piraeus under her own power and that the **HAINULT** would act as her escort. That way if it came to a fight in the arbitration court hearing, fees for escorting could also be claimed. The **CERCUR** was to be manned by the 3rd and 4th Engineers, the Mate and the 3rd Mate and three of the crew. They felt that this was just about enough, and it meant that both bridge and engine-room staff of both vessels would be working six on and six off for the best part of three days. They felt that it was expedient to pass the west coast of Crete in daylight, and decided to leave that afternoon. That day they lunched heartily, it was the last time for some days that some them were to taste Angel's sumptuous cooking, and boarded hopefully the **CERCUR** for the last time.

Both generators running, the steering gear was tested and observed to be working, and for the first time they were treated to the clang of the telegraphs working as they were swung to STAND BY. The anchors were weighed and the engine started with a gentle woomph, and the Mate rung down for SLOW AHEAD. As the engineers had no prior knowledge of what revolutions slow ahead was, they took a guess at 65 r.p.m. As there was little manoeuvring to be done this did not present a problem. As soon as they were well clear of the wadi and out into the Mediterranean, the Mate rung down for FULL AHEAD and the 3rd Engineer moved the throttle lever till there was only four notches left, and using the voice-pipe to the bridge told them that the engines were turning at 135 r.p.m. and that was flat out. (Engineers always keep a bit in reserve).

Between the engineers and the mates they decided that

FULL SPEED AHEAD	=	130 r.p.m.
HALF AHEAD	=	85
SLOW AHEAD	=	65
DEAD SLOW AHEAD	=	45/50 as they were

not sure at what revolutions the engine would stall. The two engineers were disappointed at the state of the engine-room, as during the trip toward Crete they found so many leaks particularly amongst the fuel-lines. One of the fuel lines was spraying diesel oil from a union so badly, that the 4th Engineer had to don a face mask before approaching it and tightening up the union. All the problems they encountered were caused simply by poor maintenance. Some hours later one of the crew came down to tell them that there was even hot water in the taps. In the funnel they found a waste-heat boiler and it was obviously doing its work. One of the crew had volunteered to do the cooking, but was amazed to find that although the **CERCUR** had been built in 1946 she had a coal fired galley stove. There was plenty of work for the deck-hands. The derricks had to be lowered and fettered, the old hatch-boards that were still available were put back in position and the tarpaulin battened down. The mooring ropes were coiled away and a bit of general cleaning up was done.

When this was finished the 3rd Engineer asked the Mate if he could use the men to clean up the engine and the engine-room. By the second morning the coast of Crete was sighted the **CERCUR** was beginning to look tidier and cleaner both on deck and below. The only cock-up occurred when some-one dropped some cotton waste in the bilge at the same time as it was being pumped. Minutes later the 3rd had the suction pipe off and the waste removed.

On passing the western tip of Crete Duff told Flashy to radio their ETA and for the agent to make arrangements for docking. Several hours later Flashy took up a radio message to Duff which read:-

FROM PAPADOLUS BROTHERS SHIPPING STOP ARE WILLING TO NEGOTIATE REASONABLE PRICE FOR CERCUR STOP DRY DOCK AVAILABLE AT PIRAEUS ON ENTRY STOP ALL SUBJECT TO SURVEY ENDS

Having cleared Crete they set course due north on the final leg to Piraeus. Duff requested a pilot to board the

CERCUR off Aiyina for the final approach to Piraeus. This amused the Greek authorities, who questioned their competency. "We're bringing back to Greece a Greek ship that was wrecked by a Greek captain", was Duff's ungracious reply. Although it was unusual, the Pilot vessel did travel out much farther than usual to accommodate them. The Mate rung down for DEAD SLOW AHEAD and the engine did manage to run at 45 r.p.m. without stalling. The companion ladder was lowered and up clambered four men. One was instantly recognised as Captain Spiros Gregio who easily found his way to the bridge followed by the Pilot. The next man was the Chief Engineer of the **CERCUR** and was followed by a Lloyds Surveyor James Cass. Gregio asked if he could take the wheel under the guidance of the Pilot and the Mate replied, "Be my guest, I shall be transferring to the **HAINULT** in a few minutes and Captain Duff will be Master of this vessel. You talk to him". At that moment Duff and Taffy came on board to relieve the Mate and the 4th Engineer.

Down in the engine-room the Chief Engineer, Christos Dolou was grinning when he saw how clean the engine-room was, and asked, "Why is it that you British have to have everything so clean and perfect. It's only a place to work in". "'Cause we're English", was the quick reply. Just outside the port the **HAINULT** dropped anchor and saw her charge fade into the distance. The **CERCUR** was manoeuvred into dry-dock and before the water had started pumping out the owners agents were on board and negotiation started.

Straight to the Master's cabin they all trooped, and Gregio unlocked the drinks cabinet, and asked if they would care for a drink. Duff said that he could not drink the ouzo but would have a whisky, and everybody had the same. "Mr Duff", said the agent, "I have no wish to take part in a haggling match which is the custom of my country. I compliment you on the job that you and your crew have done in bringing in the **CERCUR**. Your timely intervention prevented the **CERCUR** meeting her destruction. You have saved the best part of three-quarters of her cargo, and she does not appear to have suffered much damage. The cargo that you saved forms part of your settlement for which I have an international money voucher in my briefcase. Subject to a reasonable survey, I am empowered by the owners to offer you 25% of the value of the vessel. I do not want an answer now. An answer in the morning after next will do nicely. I bid you good-day". He tipped the contents of his glass down his throat and left.

The following morning the **CERCUR** was standing on the keel-blocks high and dry. Duff was roused by Taffy at 06:00. "I want to look at the bottom before anyone else gets here", said Taffy. They walked round the dry-dock first and noted that the rudder looked a little askew. "No wonder", said Duff, "the Mate told me that when he put the wheel amidships she steered about 3 degrees to starboard. That would explain it". "I think the stern frame is bent a bit", said Taffy, "probably bent as we pulled her off". When they descended to the floor of the dry-dock they both noted that the port bilge keel had parted company from the hull for a length of about twenty feet. They were both surprised to find that the damage to the ship's bottom was indeed slight. They counted seventeen plates that would have to be removed and faired up, and they both doubted if any would have to be replaced. "Well", said Taffy, "we got her home, anchors an' all". At 10:00 James Cass came on board and said, grinning, "I take it that you have already carried out your own survey. I wonder if it's the same as mine".

By 16:00 he had finished, and came back to the cabin, joined them for another drink, where they compared notes. James Cass had counted out nineteen plates for fairing, stern frame twisted about 3" and rudder skewed slightly. He also noted that one of the propeller blades was slightly bent. He felt that the bilge keel would have to be removed, faired up and could be put back. "A job well done, Mr Duff. My report will be typed up tonight and I will see you back here in the morning. I suggest that you phone the agents and tell them that the survey is complete.

The following morning Duff and Taffy waited in

trepidation. On board first came Gregio and his Chief Engineer to be followed minutes later by James Cass, the owners agent, and one of the Papadulos brothers. The Lloyds Surveyor gave each of them a copy of his report on the condition of the ship. Papadulos smiled and through his agent said that he felt fortunate that the repairs were minimal. The Surveyor went on to say that in his opinion the prompt action of those on the **HAINULT** had prevented the **CERCUR** being damaged still further while grounded. They had laboured long hours to save the cargo of sheep, thus maintaining the goodwill of the company in delivery of cargo. They had taken the best course, and hygienically disposed of the remainder of the sheep that had perished. The vessels holds had been completely cleaned to the extent that there were no lingering smells. He added that they had, in his opinion improved the efficiency of the engines, and last but not least, they had brought her back to her home port of Piraeus, anchors an' all. He recommended that the owners offer 35% of the ships value, plus the cheque for the cargo. Duff reminded them that they could go to a court of arbitration.

The agent and the owner left the vessel to consult with the other Papadulos Brothers, meanwhile Gregio assured them that as a fellow Greek that they would settle for 35%. The following morning the agent came on board with a letter from the Brothers, stating that they were willing to accept the recommended terms and that an international money order would be forthcoming, on receipt of which they were to vacate the vessel and hand over to Gregio. The agent handed them the money order for the cargo settlement and left. A few hours later in the afternoon he was back with the other money order for thirty-five thousand pounds sterling. Duff and Taffy bid their hasty farewells to Gregio and picked up a taxi, taking them first to the bank to lodge the money and then on the quay. A picket boat took them out to the **HAINULT**. "I bet you dears would like something to eat", said Angel. "I didn't think I could miss anyone's cooking as much as I've missed yours", said Taffy. "I try to please", said Angel.

THE U-BOAT

The following morning found them setting off for the Wadi Baacon after they had bunkered. Three days later found them anchoring in the wadi well clear of the U-boats site. "Can we get down to that depth using just scuba gear or will we have to go down in full immersion suits?" said Duff. "Let's use the work-boat and go down with full immersion suits", said Taffy. The following morning found the work-boat manoeuvred to a position above the U-boat and they were lowered over the side. Using their air controls they slowly descended to the depths. As they neared the vessel they found that it had sunk into the sand by about 3', and they wondered how on earth they could climb upon to the casing. As they slowly moved along its side they found footholds going up and over the cigar-shaped ballast tanks. The southern end of the Mediterranean Sea is not an area where seaweed grows readily, nor was there much in the way of marine growth, e.g. barnacles and the like. However they were not alone down there. As they climbed into the upper conning tower they backed out very quickly when a moray eel bared its teeth.

They moved slowly along the casing to where they knew the escape chamber was situated. The hand-wheel on top of it was corroded to the extent that the outer ring and its spokes broke off as soon as any attempt was made to turn it.

When they surfaced they discussed what course of action they could take. Taffy said, "I reckon that if you and the 2nd engineer in immersion suits go down with a big stillson wrench you might get the escape door open. If you can do that I can get inside using a scuba set with extra oxygen cylinders. I've been in a few U-boats in my time and I know my way around. I'm going to send down the 2nd with you and a dirty big stillson and hopefully when you've got the door open I'm going to pop inside the sardine can". Forty-five minutes later there was a tug on his line and he started finning his way down, using the line as a guide, to the sub laden with extra air cylinders. Down, down he went feeling the pressure building up in his head. He allowed himself to float gently into the chamber while the other two closed the lid on top of him.

Opening the drain valve, the water disappeared from the chamber in seconds. Cautiously, he tried the small watertight door, and it creaked a bit before it swung open. The inside of the U-boat was a surprise. It was tidy and totally in order. There were numerous grisly skeletons lying on the deck, some propped up against the bulkheads. He passed through two watertight doors before he came to the control-room. Here there were more skeletons some with their officers caps that had slipped down to cover the sockets that had once contained eyes. Picking up a spanner he knocked on the casing dot-dot-dot-dot-dot dash-dash. He guessed that those outside would read this as an OK message. Looking at his pressure gauge on his air cylinder he found that he had used up a lot of his air supply and very shortly he changed over to the last pair of cylinders. He spent some time with his flash-light examining the pressure gauges in the engine-room, till he found the one that he was really after. The one of the large air receiver was the one that he was particularly interested in. It registered a considerable pressure, enough for what he wanted.

Lifting up some of the plates in the control-room, he traced out the lines that he wanted. He moved again to the air receivers and opened the isolating valve. Back to the control-room to the operating valve. This was indeed stiff from lack of use and Taffy knew that this was his only chance. He had to bring the submarine to the surface as his own air supply was beginning to dwindle. As he opened the valve there was a strange whooshing sound accompanied by a creaking and groaning, and Taffy experienced a strange floating sensation as the vessel started rising from its water grave.

Those on the outside were surprised at the sudden movement and were in a bit of a quandary, not knowing whether to risk the "bends" with a speedy ascent to the surface or to jump off and rise slowly. They rashly decided on the former and clung on for dear life to the machine gun mounted aft of the conning tower. Minutes later the U-boat came to the surface, much to the relief of Taffy. When he felt the vessel gently rocking he knew the vessel was on the surface, and climbing up the ladder to the conning-tower found that he was unable to turn the hand-wheel. The continuous effort was tiring him and was reducing his air supply to the red part of his air contents gauge. Picking up a spanner he tapped out an SOS repeatedly on the side of the conning tower. The 2nd Mate heard instantly and guessed what was happening as the tapping was moving along the hull. Fortunately the 2nd Engineer still had the stillson wrench with him and this enabled him to open the conning-tower hatch from the outside. Taffy climbed out of the hatch, tearing off his face mask only collapse on the spot.

The other two still being in their diving suits could do little to help him. This was all observed from both the workboat and the **HAINULT** which quickly moved alongside. By this time Taffy had come round, and opening his eyes said drearily, "That's a helluva way to raise a sunken vessel. Taffy and the 2nd Engineer were transferred to the workboat where they stripped off their diving gear, and the **HAINULT** dropped anchor.

That evening there was a lot of conversation centring around what to do with a submarine left over from the war, that could not be used of for its intended purpose. Flashy was sending messages through the agents network, but the first two message were to the Royal Navy at Portsmouth and the German Naval Authorities. The Germans speedily sent the reply that the U-boat was an official war grave and as such should be left undisturbed. Duff relayed the message that they had already carried out the salvage operations (neglecting to say how) and already had the submarine on the surface. This put the Germans in a bit of a quandary. The following message came through a few days later:-

TO MASTER HAINULT FROM GERMAN NAVAL

COMMAND BREMERHAVEN STOP AMERICAN DESTROYER ARCHIMEDES WILL BE WITH YOU IN THREE DAYS TIME STOP NAVAL PERSONNEL WILL REMOVE BODIES FROM VESSEL AND TAKE THEM BACK TO GERMANY STOP.

There was no mention of any payment so they assumed that there was none forthcoming. No-one seemed interested in buying a submarine, so it seemed to Duff that they could only sell it for scrap, and the nearest ship-breakers were in Turkey. The radio started buzzing away to agents to arrange a sale to Turkish breakers and within a day, a ship-breaker agreed to buy the sub at a price that covered all their costs from the time that they had left Piraeus with a small profit, but Duff was still a bit peeved. However the following day the **ARCHIMEDES** radioed to say that her ETA was four hours thence. The **HAINULT** weighed anchor and took the U-boat outside the shelter of the wadi into deeper water and anchored again. Over the horizon came the **ARCHIMEDES** and close by were two ocean going tugs as well. The **ARCHIMEDES** anchored a full half a mile distant and a cutter was very quickly lowered into the water before setting off for the **HAINULT**. The Captain stepped on board the **HAINULT** and said "In the morning my men will be coming over the submarine to remove all the bodies, and paperwork. We thank-you for your co-operation, but we will be taking over from now". "Tell me Captain", said Duff, "what are the two tugs for?" "To take her back to the States", he said "You can't do that", said Duff, "she's already sold to a Turkish breaker". "Then unsell her", was the reply, "I am empowered to settle with you for a one-off payment of $500,000. I am sorry but this figure is non-negotiable.

The following morning the individual remains of each body were carefully laid to rest in separate boxes and taken on board the American vessel. Taffy ventured back on to the submarine and was surprised at what a good airing had done to the atmosphere inside. The American Captain asked him if he had attempted to run the engines of the submarine and about the general condition of the vessel. Taffy advised against starting the engine as he reckoned that many of the joints would have rotted in the time that the sub had been on the bottom and any extra pressure such as starting would have a tendency to blow the joints. Taffy said that the diesel oil in the lines had probably turned to jelly anyway. The batteries were complete flat, and Taffy having brought her to the surface had exhausted what air she had had in her receivers.

They had found the U-boat's Captains cabin. The Captain had been Fritz Wolfgang, and in her log-book, the Captain had kept a record of the last patrol. It stated how he had sunk two heavily loaded coasters just outside Alexandria and how he had crept stealthily into Tobruk harbour and torpedoed a tanker and a loaded troop transport. He managed to get out of the harbour but was chased by a destroyer till he drew level with the wadi. At that time he spotted another destroyer that was heading towards him. He decided on the action which, in the end was to defeat him, and turned into the wadi at periscope depth When in the wadi he sat the vessel on the bottom, fortunately they were not depth-charged but the continuous movement of vessels in the wadi warned the Captain that they would be in considerable danger if they attempted to flee the wadi. The crew of the U-boat decided to sit it out, but the oxygen content was diminishing. Some of the crew were hallucinating, and for safety sake lay down to best conserve what oxygen they could, but within days they were all dead. It was all in the log, and it was noticed that the writing was becoming more feeble as each page was turned.

THE PAPA D

Before the **HAINULT** had left Alexandria they had the promise of towing a coaster from Piraeus to Malta. Flashy got in touch with the agent and asked him to find out if the offer was still good as many months had passed. The agent informed them that the offer was still available on "daily hire" basis only. They accepted the offer on the spot, and they were given instructions on where to find the vessel. Sailing to Piraeus they rounded the Greek coast and spotted her. She was in a sorry state, and was lying on a beach, sitting on the bottom. She was a 500 ton coaster by the name of **PAPA D**, and had been built in 1913. She had had her engine and rudder removed and had been beached for the last two years because she leaked so badly. She was holed in both holds, but her engine-room space was said to be water-tight. At the time that she had been beached had been used as a barge. Her bridge had also been removed to provide more deck space, and she had not been inspected. A Maltese company, however, being short of vessels, had decided to buy her, re-engine her, and press her into service.

The **HAINULT** went alongside and put her hoses into the holds and for hours all eyes were watching to see if she would float. Many hours later she did start to float but her after end stayed well down. They had been told that the "engine-room" was not holed, but nevertheless it still contained an enormous amount of water. Once the vessel was well afloat she was anchored using her own anchor. The **HAINULT** continued pumping till there was only a foot of water in the holds. It was noted however that the level of water rose steadily by about 6" per hour in both holds. Duff turned his attention to the "engine-room" and started pumping. This space was a small one and did not take long to pump down to the level of the tank tops. It was then found that when the engine had been removed, so too had the tailshaft. The gaping hole left by the tailshaft had been blanked off with a piece of plywood at both ends and held in position with a length of studding. Due to its long immersion in sea-water both boards had rotted away, and the studding though badly corroded still lay in the stern tube. Taffy was over the side with his snorkel and mask and a wooden ruler in his hand, and in no time he was back on board. Chippy started fashioning a tapered bung that he said could be banged into the hole. Several hours later, with the "engine-room" flooded again, Taffy was over the side with a line, tied to the bung. Down he went, and as they all watched from the deck, the wooden bung disappeared from the surface, only minutes later to reappear with Taffy again. "Someone give 'us a hand", he said, "The bung keeps pulling me up". Down went Duff, and between them they pushed the bung into the stern tube. When they came up Duff said, "Why didn't you take the hammer down with you?" Taffy replied, "In a few minutes that wood will swell so much, that you'll be lucky if you ever get it out". "Then why don't you get Chippy to do the same with all the other holes in the hull?" "The hull is so rotten that if we put wood into the holes the plates will buckle", said Taffy.

Climbing back on board the **HAINULT**, they transferred the hoses back to the "engine-room" and pumped it dry. Sure enough from then onwards no water entered.

They decided that it would be prudent to lash the **PAPA D** alongside rather than tow her. By doing this they could keep an eye on the water level in the holds and pump them when necessary. At 04:00 the pumps were started again and the coaster was pumped down, and the crew using crowbars turned the rusty old windlass and raised the anchor. By breakfast time they were on their way.

Chippy on the other hand had had a brainwave, and, with one of the crew had gone down into the hold, and the pair of them standing waist high in water laboured to put a wide plank in position over one of the holes and braced it from the deckhead. This stemmed the flow of water considerably, and, still having the sweet smell of success did the same in the after hold.

The hold was pumped down completely and it was found

that the vessel was only making about an inch of water an hour. This was a relief, as the **HAINULT** could now tow **the PAPA D** instead of having her alongside. It did mean that they might have to stop every twelve hours to see what water was making its way into the vessel. A medium towing cable was manhandled on to the forecastle of the coaster and made fast, and the **HAINULT** cast off and brought her stern level with the **PAPA D's** bow where the eye was brought back on board the **HAINULT** and put on to her towing hook. Sufficient cable was pulled out till the distance between them was about fifty yards. They were able to work up to a towing speed of about six knots by the time they had cleared the Greek Islands.

Chippy's efforts were well worthwhile and in the four days that it took them to reach Valletta they only had to stop twice to reduce the water level in the holds. The **PAPA D** was quickly pulled up on to a waiting slip-way after the holds were pumped again. Later the survey revealed that it would found that she was not worth repairing and she was scrapped while she sat on the slip-way.

ADMIRALTY TOW

A radio message informed them of the offer of "daily hire only" to tow two Admiralty tugs from Bizerta (in Tunisia) to Portsmouth. For a long time the port of Bizerta had been used as a Mediterranean Royal Navy base. Now that the base was being evacuated the tugs were surplus to requirements and were to be decommissioned on arrival at Portsmouth. After bunkering at Valletta they set off for Bizerta, which was three days sailing. After bunkering again, it was decided to lash an Admiralty tug either side of the **HAINULT** rather than tow astern. If they had towed astern each of the tugs would have had to be manned. Duff decided that the small sacrifice in speed was worth the extra safety that was gained by lashing either side. The trio set off the following morning and by noon had worked up to a speed of nearly six knots. They found that any change in course had to be made very slowly. One evening they found caviar on the menu. When Angel was asked how it suddenly appeared on the menu, his simple reply was, "I didn't feel that the Admiralty would need it any more on their tugs". They were treated to a few more of Angel's delicacies before they bunkered at Tangiers twelve days later. The long haul up the coast of Portugal followed. On reaching the Spanish port of La Coruna they bunkered for the passage through the Bay of Biscay. They were fortunate that throughout this passage they were blessed with good weather. On approaching Ushant (W. France) at night they ran into dense fog. They heard Ushant's fog signal but were unable to see the beam from the lighthouse, so a course was set for Eddystone Rock. By 06:00 the fog had lifted and there was Eddystone Rock fine on the starboard bow.

Flashy radioed in to Portsmouth for docking tugs to bring in the Admiralty tugs individually. Neither of them had steam on board, and it was impossible to anchor them. Within hours the **HAINULT** anchored off Selsey Bill to await the arrival of the tugs. A couple of hours later the tugs arrived and took their charges in tow, only then could the **HAINULT** enter Portsmouth to bunker for the trip to Falmouth to enjoy a well-earned rest and spot of leave. A day later found them tying up in the harbour at Falmouth and the crew leaving the vessel, but not so for Taffy. He shut the boilers down as soon as he could, he had repairs that were overdue and he had made arrangements to change over the boilers from coal-firing to oil-firing. This meant that the coal bunker spaces had to be scrupulously cleaned and the openings plated up. Connection to these tanks had to be made on deck for bunkering purposes. In the engine-room itself the furnace fronts had to be exchanged for the new ones before the pipe-work and new pumps could be installed. Now it meant that the range of the **HAINULT** could be almost doubled and only one stoker per watch would be needed.

The boilers badly needed a descale, as they had used south Mediterranean water that had a high salinity. One of the winches had been strained slightly in pulling off the **CERCUR** and he wanted to check out the windlass himself. Angel insisted on staying on board, he said that the **HAINULT** was home to him anyway, he didn't have anywhere else to go and had no relations. "Besides", he said, "I've got to look after Chiefy". "Don't call me Chiefy", said Taffy.

Within a week or two all the crew were back with the exception of a couple of seamen, and the shore gangs of fitters had completed all their work. Taffy announced that the boilers were in better working order than they had every been. The windlass had been re-aligned and the winch had been taken ashore and repaired, and was now back in place. Taffy had brought the boilers up to a full head of steam each day and the engine was warmed through each day in readiness for the call that they hoped would bring them work. For days they sat and waited. Flashy, as ever, sat by the radio, scanning the wave-bands in search of distress calls. For three weeks they just sat there till Duff and Taffy began to wonder if they should pay the crew off. By this time the weather had become changeable and on some days some of the ships laid-up in the River Fal dragged their anchors. Late one evening Flashy rushed to Duff's cabin with a flimsy. At once Taffy and the engineers flashed up the boilers, and put the steam on to start warming through the engine. The message read:-

MAYDAY MAYDAY FROM MASTER SS SANTIAGO BAY POS 49 1ON 7 24W STOP HAVE LOST PROPELLER STOP AM WITHOUT POWER AND DRIFTING NE STOP REQUIRE EARLIEST TUG ASSISTANCE STOP FORCE EIGHT GALE BLOWING FROM SW STOP ACKNOWLEDGE.

Duff estimated that the **HAINULT** could run at an average speed of eight knots. Flashy radioed the **SANTIAGO BAY** telling them that they would be arriving at the scene in about fourteen hours. A return message came back.

MASTER SANTIAGO BAY TO MASTER HAINULT STOP LOOK FORWARD TO MEETING YOU STOP HURRY

As they cleared Falmouth they met the teeth of a terrific gale often gusting force nine. This however was the weather that the **HAINULT** was built to withstand, but not at a speed of 10 knots. Taffy cut the engine revs to a speed of about six and a half knots to save wear and tear on the tailshaft. The **HAINULT** bounced through the waves and many a time there was from eight to ten inches of water slopping across the decks. The **HAINULT** was adequately scuppered and always shook herself free of the water,. After four or more hours the gale suddenly abated and Duff rung down for more revolutions, and as she reached a higher speed Duff asked Taffy if he could raise even more revs as he didn't want to be late in arriving at the scene. For hours they raced up and over the waves, but at the point when they were within twenty miles of the **SANTIAGO BAY**, the heavens opened and another gale blew up to about force eight, once again forcing them to lower their speed. Two hours later found them within sight of the **SANTIAGO BAY**.

Several attempts were made before a messenger line was finally got on board. A heavy messenger line was brought across and as soon as the main towing cable was slipped over the stern of the **HAINULT** the heavy messenger parted. It was fourteen hours before the **SANTIAGO BAY** finally managed to shackle up the towing cable to its anchor. Little by little Duff inched the **SANTIAGO BAY** round on to a course that would take her back to Falmouth. The **SANTIAGO BAY** was difficult to control as she took on an uncontrollable shear, as her steering gear had broken down and her rudder was swinging freely from side to side. Once Duff had got on course the engineers on the **SANTIAGO BAY** lashed up the steering gear quadrant midships and this at least made the going easier. They met the same calm patch that they had met outward bound and for a few hours were able to make 6 knots.

A few miles past the Scilly Isles brought them back into the bad weather again and Duff had to reduce speed to about 3 knots. They counted their blessing that the wind was behind them and for many hours they crawled up and down the waves. When they had reached Mounts Bay two gigantic waves one after the other swamped the **HAINULT** and as the water cleared they could see the towing cable hanging directly down from the stern. It was quickly winched in while this was being done Duff was inching the tug as near to the **SANTIAGO BAY** as he dared so that another messenger could be fired across. Although there was still a very high sea running the first attempt was successful and within two hours they were under way again. This time the **HAINULT** really had to pull the stops out, to prevent the **SANTIAGO BAY** drifting in close to the shore and had to steer on a large arc before getting back on course. As the **HAINULT** rounded Lizzard Point they entered the lee side of the storm and into calmer waters. At least now they were safe, but Flashy rushed up the bridge with another flimsy for Duff, it read:-

XXX SOS FROM MASTER CHIGWELL LODGE STOP CREW ABANDONING SHIP POS 49 2ON 6 OOW STOP WILL ACCEPT LLOYDS OPEN FORM ENDS

Duff told Flashy to radio back and ask what condition the vessel was in. Back came the reply that the vessel had a 30 degree list to starboard, two of her holds were flooding due to the loss of her hatch covers and her boiler-room was flooded up to the furnaces. She had heavy deck cargo and movement of this had brought down the foremast. Flashy radioed back to say that when they had dropped their charge at Falmouth and bunkered they would be attempting to reach the **CHIGWELL LODGE**.

The next message was to Falmouth requesting their bunkering needs be met, (at least it could now be completed in an hour). They required two new towing cables to be on the quay waiting for them and they requested docking tugs to meet the **SANTIAGO BAY** as soon as she entered Falmouth Bay. As good as their word the docking tugs met them just beyond the mouth of the Helford River. The **HAINULT**'s cable was brought in and the docking tugs took over. This allowed the **HAINULT** to go at full speed into Falmouth. There were the cables waiting for them on the quay and as soon as they tied up the derrick was raised and the cables were lowered into the hold. At the same time a small bunkering tanker came alongside the snaking hoses pumped her bunkers till she was full and replenished her water supply. Angel had been kept busy making sure his stores were replenished. "First salvage we've made where my stores didn't benefit", was all he said. Within two and a half hours they had cleared Falmouth Bay and in the course of doing this were in time to see the **SANTIAGO BAY** enter the bay.

THE CHIGWELL LODGE

Round the Lizard Point and they began to battle the elements again and yet again had to reduce speed. They set a course of 225 degrees which should have taken to the **CHIGWEL LODGE**'s last position. For hours Flashy had been trying to raise the vessel on the radio, all to no avail. Several hours later they reached the original position for the **CHIGWELL LODGE** but there was no sign of her. For three hours they carried out a systematic grid pattern search, then Flashy announced that there was a continuous blip on the radio, and as he moved the antenna round he found that he got a clearer signal when it was facing east. Duff decided to move towards the east and begin a systematic grid search there. The weather was still gusting up to 70 mph and the waves most of the time rose to a height of twenty feet. The sky was leaden and their progress was very slow. An hour or so later they sighted the **CHIGWELL LODGE** and what a sorry state she was in. They began to search for survivors, to no avail.

Although she had a list of 30 degrees the buffeting of the sea often made her heel over to 45 degrees so that her starboard deck rails were awash, and waves were continuously washing into the open No1. hold. On deck there had been four steam locomotives each weighing about 70 tons that had been secured with steel chains that had been welded to the deck. The locomotives that had originally been on the port side had received the full force of the gale, and the gale had either stretched the chains beyond their limit or the locos had worked loose, or the welding of the chains to the deck has been defective. Whatever the cause these two locomotives had gone over the side, tearing great chunks of the bulwarks away from the ships side, leaving them sticking out like fins. As they drew close, those on deck peered through binoculars and scanned her. The 3rd Mate jumped for joy when he spotted someone on the poop deck.

Duff brought the **HAINULT** in close the stricken vessel so that they could shout across to each other. The Captain's name was Austin and he spoke with a broad highland accent, "I knew you would come", he said. He had rigged life-lines across the after deck as well as across the foredeck, as there was no possibility of moving along the port rails. They had disappeared when the locos had gone over the side.

Duff and Taffy weighed up the situation with regard to the towing. Captain Austin informed them that the rudder was midships, so it made sense to tow the **CHIGWELL LODGE** from the bows but how on earth were they to get a tow-rope on board?

It took over an hour for Captain Austin to reach the forecastle. Several time he was washed off his feet, only to be saved by the life-line. When he reached the forecastle he tied himself to the hand-wheels of the windlass for safety sake. Once in position a light messenger line was fired over the forecastle. This was repeated many times but he was unable to reach them although he now had both hands free, because he was lashed in a fixed position and they landed out of reach. On the seventh attempt the line fell directly over his shoulder and he was able to start hauling in the line. The vessel was lurching badly and he wound the line round the drum of the windlass. On several occasions the forecastle pitched so badly that it went right under and on one occasion when she came up there was the Captain laying prone and apparently lifeless. Duff manoeuvred **the HAINULT** dangerously close till she was feet away from the vessels side and the mate, Bill Samuels took a flying leap on to the slanting deck of the **CHIGWELL LODGE**. He slithered down the deck and was caught by the ships rail just as a wave broke over the vessel. As the water ran out of the scuppers the Mate stood up and waved. By this time the **HAINULT** was running hard astern. It was noticed that Captain Austin was now on his feet and had thrown a rope down the deck to the Mate. The Mate pulled himself up the sloping deck and made himself fast to the life-line and very gingerly made his way up to the forecastle where he was joined by the Captain. A shot of rum from his hip flask revived them both and they were able to start heaving in the heavier messenger line. The pair of them knew that it would be a nearly impossible feat to bring aboard the heavy eye of the main towing cable. When they could see the eye beneath the bow they decided it was time for a meal and a rest as they were both reaching the point of exhaustion. Hand over hand they made their way back to the midships accommodation where the Captain raided the galley stored for tinned food. Meanwhile the Mate took the dangerous step of descending into the engine-room. He found that the boilers still had a pressure of 60lbs. Having found this bit of joyous news he opened the valve to deck steam and hoped that there were no fractures in the steam lines. A meal was made out of corned beef and tinned peaches but what both of them really wanted was a cup of tea. Both refreshed, they left the accommodation, and slowly made their way down to the foredeck. By this time the starboard deck rails were permanently under water, and they guessed that the list had increased to 40 degrees. Captain Austin ventured down the sloping deck to open the deck steam isolating valve that was situated immediately in front of the bridge and the Mate held him steady by means of a line. Slowly he made his way up and even more slowly they made their way towards the forecastle.

The Mate opened the drain-cocks on the windlass cylinders and opened the steam valve. Water gushed out. He was ever mindful that he was wasting precious steam but did not want to smash the cylinders by the ingress of water. At last a whisper of steam emerged from the drain cocks and this was the signal that they could be shut. Within minutes the windlass was turning albeit slowly but it was enough to raise the main towing cable. When they had three turns round the drum they paid out sufficient on to the deck to enable it to be lifted over a bollard. The eye was slithering around the deck and they had to pick their moment to pick up the eye and drop it over the bollard. Knowing that they would both require two free hands to work with they lashed themselves to the bollard with about four feet of spare rope. As they eye dropped over the bollard it pulled the lifelines so severely that it brought them both to their knees.

At last the tow could begin. Unfortunately it was necessary to take a turn to starboard. If the **HAINULT** had attempted this the **CHIGWELL LODGE** would certainly have capsized. For the next two hours the **HAINULT** gently turned through 270 degrees before setting course for Falmouth. The **CHIGWELL LODGE** was still shipping enormous seas and both Duff and Captain Austin agreed that the two remaining locomotives would have to go over the side before there was any reasonable chance of getting her home. The mate, Bill Samuels and Captain Austin raided the engine-room stores and found a couple of hacksaws and search as they did they could find no more than six blades. The following morning the weather abated slightly and they made the perilous journey down the sloping deck to where the chains were welded to the deck. They lashed themselves on guy lines from the hatch coamings, and also tied a length of string on to the hacksaws so that they could not be lost. The diameter of the metal that comprised each link was nearly an inch. Captain Austin took the rear and Bill Samuels took the front and they both started sawing through the chain links. After cutting part way through, an extra large wave swept them off their feet and jarred them so badly that the first pair of blades broke and they were thankful that they had not lost the hacksaws altogether. When they only had about quarter of an inch to go, the rolling of the vessel put so much strain on the links that they started opening up. Both of them climbed up the sloping deck again to wait for the vessel to roll again. Each time the vessel rolled the links opened up a bit more, till in the end the links sprung wide open and the locomotive slide down the remainder of the deck smashing away the bulwark before tipping over the side. When this happened they could hear the cheer from the **HAINULT**.

The **CHIGWELL LODGE** straightened herself up a bit and the list decreased to about 25 degrees. Captain Austin felt that it would be prudent to also get rid of the remaining loco, but decided to leave this operation till the following morning. Fortunately the following morning greeted them with an improvement in the weather, at least the wind had died down. Another meal of corned beef and tinned peaches, and the pair of them lashed themselves again by means of guy ropes before they started sawing. An hour later the links were sawn through completely, but still the loco sat firmly on the deck. The weather was continuing to improve to the extent that the vessel was barely rolling. Duff gave a lot of thought before he took the decision to pull the vessel sharply to starboard so that she would heel slightly and tip the deck enough for the loco to topple. It worked successfully and the **HAINULT** resumed course. The **CHIGWELL LODGE** rolled up till she only had a list of 10 degrees.

At least it was easier to move about on deck. By late afternoon the **HAINULT** came alongside and with her hoses put steam on board to pump out her boiler-room. When this was complete, steam was kept on for a few hours to operate the fuel heating and the fuel-oil pumps. Once a sufficient head of steam had been raised the boiler-room could be self sufficient and Taffy went on board. The **HAINULT** continued towing easily and Taffy in the meantime managed to raise a full head of steam and started to warm through the main engine and started pumping out the water in the other holds, he already had the generator running as well as the steering gear in operation. While he was occupied in the engine-room Captain Austin was watching the water level in No.1 hold gradually subside. Some of the drums in No.1 hold were just becoming exposed above the water level and from them came a whiff of hydrogen and as some of them became even more exposed the outside of the drums started steaming. The Captain rung down on the deck telephone and told Taffy to stop pumping the hold and come aloft. The **HAINULT** came alongside and several of the seamen were transferred to the **CHIGWELL LODGE**. All the hatch covers were removed from No.1 hold and the derricks were rigged so that any damaged drums could be jettisoned. One by one the drums that were punctured or showed signs of damage were raised from the hold and dropped over the side. On numerous occasions, underwater explosions that resembled depth charges were heard. These caused concern to Taffy, and he asked what was in the drums? "Sodium", said Captain Austin. "I didn't think that was a dangerous cargo", said Taffy. "It's not normally", said the captain, "But this is sodium metal. It is stored in paraffin, and when exposed to air it burns with terrific heat and becomes explosive when in contact with water". "Blimey", said Taffy. As soon as the offending drums had been removed Taffy continued with the pumping of the hold and the seamen stayed down there to watch for any more suspect drums. This was a prudent move as a few more were found and these were disposed of in the same way. The hold was pumped dry and then Taffy pumped the other holds, although there was very little in them. By this time the main steam was on to the engine and it was decided that for the remaining 20 or 30 miles the **CHIGWELL LODGE** could make her own way to Falmouth. Removing the towing eye from the bollard was easy with so many hands available and the **HAINULT** was able to take it back on board and stow it away. It wasn't till the **CHIGWELL LODGE** was safely tied up that Taffy learnt that the after holds contained iron ingots and dynamite. "Like a floating time-bomb", said Taffy.

 The captain of the **CHIGWELL LODGE** inquired whether any survivors had been found and was told that a passing vessel had picked up a lifeboat with seven suvivors, who had been placed in hospital with exposure.

THE CHEYNEY

The **CHIGWELL LODGE** actually berthed before the **HAINULT**. When the authorities found out what her cargo consisted of she was docked in the outer harbour away from the other vessels. Before she could proceed with her voyage her cargo in the forward holds was restowed. Alas the **HAINULT** was only spared for a couple of days before she was asked to proceed to Portsmouth to begin towing one of the tugs that she had previously brought there from Bizerta. Apparently one of them had been bought by The Suez Canal Company and was required at Alexandria. The **HAINULT** was contracted on daily hire for the trip to Alexandria and was promised a return tow to the UK. Angel was a bit peeved that he had to take on stores for the whole of the trip, and he knew that there was nothing of any use to him on the tug as he had already ransacked its larder.

By this time Duff had decided that he and Taffy should expand the business. They had made a lot of money and the way business was going there would be a long term need for ocean towage and ocean salvage. With this in mind they decided to take a trip off, and promote the Mate and 2nd Engineer. Both of them were more than capable of undertaking the towing to Alexandria.

The **HAINULT** took up her tow and started on the first leg of her trip to Alexandria. Meanwhile Duff and Taffy journeyed up to the Tyne to visit some of the shipyards that specialised in building tugs, to see what there was on offer. On the slip-ways of Rennoldsons was an immense craft looking resplendent, although only partly completed and painted in red oxide. The manager informed them that the vessel was being built for a Russian port and had strengthened bows to combat the icing-up of the northern ports. She was twin-screwed, diesel with hydraulic couplings to each screw. At the fore end of each main engine were enormous pumps that were salvage pumps. The inlet to each of them was 8" in diameter. The engine-room was to be equipped with a small machine shop that included a lathe, milling machine and a drill press. She had a vast hold that was to hold a multitude of devices and equipment that would prove invaluable in salvage operations. They were shown plans of the vessels and Taffy wanted to know what the long spouts were on the bridge. They looked like guns. "Fire fighting nozzles", said the manager. Those salvage pumps in the engine-room can push so much water through those nozzles that you can fight a fire at 200 feet way from the blaze, and they can be operated from inside the bridge. The bridge can be totally enclosed and will have its own independent air supply. This really is the ultimate in deep sea tugs. It is to be equipped with radar, and echo sounders and the very latest in radio equipment and direction finders". How long will it take to build?" said Duff. "Twenty-one months from keel to launch". "Put us down for two", said Duff and Taffy together. They arranged a bankers draft for the deposit, and set about booking a passage to France.

They had decided that the **HAINULT** would undoubtedly make a call at Tangiers to bunker, as it was a tax-free port, and an obvious place to meet up with them. The ferry took them across to Cherbourg where they were able to take sleeping cars on a train that took them through Paris and down to Bordeaux. The railway trip between Bordeaux and Madrid took a further three days due to continual breakdowns of the engine. From Madrid a further two days by a variety of coaches found them entering Lisbon. They were disappointed to find that the ferry that ran from Lisbon to Tangiers had departed that morning and that they had a further three-day wait before they could join it. They took the opportunity of buying a small crate that they loaded up with fruit. Later they joined the ferry and it made its way toward Tangiers.

A few hours before they docked at Tangiers, in the far distance they could just see the **HAINULT** with her tow, but somehow she looked different, she had grown another two masts. Very late that evening the **HAINULT** with her charge dropped anchor outside Tangiers and Duff and Taffy and the crate of fruit from Lisbon were rowed out to the **HAINULT**. "What have we got here me dears?" said Angel. "Something for us all to eat", said Taffy, "and don't call me dear". "OK Chiefy", said Angel. "And don't call me Chiefy".

On the outboard side lashed to the **HAINULT** was a wooden schooner. "Where did you find that?" said Duff. "Out in the bay of Biscay", said the Mate. "Why the hell did you bring it all the way here", said Taffy. "Get a better price for it here", was the Mate's answer. It transpired that they had passed Ushant and met the bad weather that everyone associates with the Bay of Biscay, and a day later is had calmed and was like a mill-pond. As they rounded the southern coast of Portugal on the last leg towards Tangiers they had spotted the masts of the schooner and made their way to her. Her decks were nearly awash but strangely she did not appear to be taking in any water. They had lashed her alongside the **HAINULT** and put hoses into her hold and started pumping her. Her cargo was motor tyres and this prevented them from pumping the hold completely dry. They were able to pump a considerable amount of water out of the hold and although she was riding higher in the water she still appeared heavy. The hoses were put into the small engine-room and that too was pumped dry, just as they anchored. The schooner was indeed a strange vessel. She had no name or number on her. The screw-holes were visible where the vessel's nameplate and identification number had been above the bridge, and someone had gone to a lot of trouble to eradicate the names on the bows and stern. There was witness that the identification had been scraped off and re-painted.

The **HAINULT** bunkered and watered so that she could continue on her journey to Alexandria. Meanwhile Duff and Taffy had decided that they would stay with the schooner to effect a sale. Noon the next day found the **HAINULT** sailing, leaving the pair to catch up with them later.

The schooner had a small compound expansion engine with a single boiler that was coal-fired. Taffy noted that the water in the boiler was towards the bottom of the gauge-glasses, so that steam could be raised for a short while to complete the pumping of the hold. Duff in the meantime was inspecting the sails that were neatly furled, and was searching for a cargo manifest. Her lifeboats had disappeared. He did however find charts that were marked out for a course to Tangiers. Obviously they had brought the vessel to the right place, and someone would be expecting their cargo. Taffy slowly steamed up the boiler, "Back breaking work", he said as he shovelled coal into the furnace, "long time since I handled a shovel". Within hours he had pumped the hold dry, but still she appeared relatively low in the water. The following morning found a motor-boat approaching the schooner and on board were two well dressed gentlemen complete with bowler hats. In Tangiers they looked completely out of place. Climbing on board, they asked for the captain, and Duff introduced himself. "We have come to collect our cargo of tyres, the vessel is a separate deal". For the next two hours Taffy was grinning like a Cheshire cat while Duff haggled over a price till one was finally agreed. Unfortunately neither Duff nor Taffy had any idea how many tyres there were in the hold. In the end they had settled for a pound a tyre. That afternoon a small craft tug brought a small lighter alongside and deposited 5 cwt of coal on the deck of the schooner and pumped some water into the schooner's water tank. Taffy fired up the boiler again, and both he and Duff spent the next hour shovelling coal down the hatch into the coal bunker. The boiler's water level was pumped up and a full head of steam was raised.

Between them, using the winch, they raised the single derrick to enable them to discharge the cargo. Taffy noticed that whenever steam was pulled from the boiler, that the boiler pressure dropped by about 5lbs. This he took as a bad sign, poor boiler condition. By early evening everything was ready for discharging cargo. They had a small meal that evening but quickly lost their appetite when they found that every thing they touched including food had a thin film of coal dust on it. The following morning local labour arrived to assist in the unloading. Taffy had taken soundings and found that there was only 4" of water in the hold. All morning they and the Arab lads toiled till the tyres had been removed. The Arab lads were down in the hold of the lighter stowing the tyres leaving Taffy loading the tyres into a cargo net and Duff controlling the winch. So they never came on board the schooner.

As he cleared the tyres, large wooden crates came to light, there were no labels on them. As soon as all the tyres were out, Duff and Taffy replaced the hatch covers to prevent any prying eyes seeing them. Early evening found the craft tug returning to take the lighter shore-side. Once they saw that the lighter was tied up in the distance, they both climbed down the ladder into the hold with lanterns in their hands. Taffy opened one of the crates with a crowbar to find that it was filled with service style machine guns. No wonder the schooner had be laying so low in the water. A passing boat was hailed to give Duff a lift to shore where he contacted the port authorities and explained what they had found and their very existence in Tangiers.

He left the Harbour Authority Office under guard and purchased an inflatable dinghy and then rowed his escort and himself back to the schooner. Within minutes the harbour-master complete with police were on board the schooner and minutes later a tug was alongside with its derrick raised. The tug had several cargo lights that were used to illuminate the schooner's deck. The first case was examined by the police and, using the derrick, hoisted the case up out of the hold and on to the tugs deck. There were three other cases in the hold and these were found to contain guns, ammunition and explosives and, these too found their way on to the deck of the tug. By now the schooner was riding high in the water, and there appeared to be only about 6" of water in the bottom of the hold.

The escort left with the tug and left Duff and Taffy looking down at a now empty hold. In the morning Taffy decided that as there was still steam in the boiler he would pump out the remaining water from the hold, and went down into the cramped engine-room to put the pump into operation while Duff was down in the hold. Duff noticed that as the water level was rapidly dropping, that there were a few bricks laying in the bottom of the hold, but they were unusual as they did not have parallel sides. On attempting to move them he found that he could not pick them up, and called down to Taffy to look at them. "They're only ballast weights", said Taffy, kicking them irritably. "Then why is there only six of them?" said Duff. As he kicked one it move slightly and between them they lifted it up and found that it was a gold ingot with assay markings from South Africa. They didn't have much sleep that night, they were too excited, and Duff remembered his Father's words, "There's gold in a boats bottom".

In the evening Taffy said, "You get rid of the gold, I'm going to sort out that boiler", and using the blow-down valve he emptied the boiler. There was no more that he could do now till Duff got back. Up he went on deck, to have a good lazy day. That night Duff still hadn't returned and Taffy had another sleepless night. He must have dozed off however, because he was awakened by a boat scraping along the side of the schooner. It was Duff and the two bowler hats. Taffy, on seeing them for the second time became suspicious. Why would people who bought motor tyres also be interested in buying gold. Taffy forever cautious, told them that before they came on board that they would have to strip of all their clothes down to vest and pants. "Don't be daft Taff", said Duff. "Have you checked to see if they are armed", said Taffy. "No", said Duff. The two bowler hats stripped off all their clothes and came on board and went down into the hold. As soon as they saw the ingots they nodded their approval and came up on deck. A bankers draft for sixty thousand pounds sterling was given to Duff as soon as they had dressed themselves. The ingots were carefully lowered into the boat. No. 1 bowler hat asked Duff if he would care to make another trip from Amsterdam to Tangiers for them. Duff declined the offer. "We are only dealers, said bowler hat No. 2. "In what", said Taffy.

Silence reigned for a few moments, then bowler hat No.2 said, "Subject to a trial run we will buy the schooner **CHEYNEY** from you for a further seven thousand pounds sterling. I'm sure she can do a few more trips for us. By the way what happened to the other part of the cargo?" Again silence reigned.

The following day Taffy went ashore in the dinghy to buy certain chemicals for the boiler, and to make arrangements for water to be delivered to the schooner for the next four mornings. Using the tankers pumps, the boiler was filled and the chemicals added in the process. The boiler was fired up and brought to a full head of steam. Early next morning Taffy blew the boiler down thus removing all the salts and debris, prior to refilling. This exercise was repeated for the next few days, till Taffy was satisfied. On the last day the boiler was flashed up and steam was put through to the engine. After a short warming through, Taffy let Duff know that all was ready, and, between them they raised the anchor. There was no telegraph between bridge and engine-room just a voice pipe. Taffy was surprised to find that the engine was in particularly good condition although it had been immersed in sea-water. His only comment to Duff was "Runs like a sewing machine". Duff took the **CHEYNEY** out into the bay and then brought her into the quay where they tied up. Duff leapt ashore and made for the nearest telephone. Within half an hour the two bowler hats were aboard and the bankers draft was in Duffs hand. "No need to take us for a boat trip", said bowler hat No.1, "we've been watching you through binoculars". "We are sailing off now", said bowler hat No.2, be so good as to cast us off". As they moved away from the quay Taffy shouted to them, "By the way you've only got enough coal for an hours steaming".

THE REST OF THE TRIP

From Tangiers they were able to take a flight to Tunis. But there were no flights eastwards from there. They were able to charter a light plane in Tunis that would take them on to Cairo. Because of the length of the flight, they had to refuel at a military base in Benghazi. After leaving Benghazi they asked the pilot to fly along the coast, where they were able to see the Wadi Baacon, where they had freed the **CERCUR** from her rocky prison. An hour or so later they saw the **HAINULT** chugging her way with her tow towards Alexandria. In the evening two days later, the **HAINULT** entered Alex, and Duff and Taffy motored out to meet them. Angel greeted them with, "Whose my lucky boys then". Flashy said to them, "Have a look at all these flimsies, boy, have people been after you. The first one is from Rennoldsons on the Tyne. The Russians have pulled out of the tug deal, and they are offering you the tug. There is a progress report on the next tug. There is a contract to tow naval vessels to the U.S. and Canada". "Send a message to Rennoldsons, said Duff, "telling them that if the offer is still on, we accept the Russian tug and cancel the building of the third. I doubt if they've even started building it. Ask them when the Ruskie will be ready. Accept the contract for the transatlantic towing. We are now in a position where we now need more work to fill the books. The **HAINAULT** delivered her charge, they bunkered and Angel was able to replenish some of his stocks. They then looked at their next towing charge. It was a floating crane of the non-propelled type. "Looks a bit top-heavy to me", said Taffy, "hope its well insured". "Don't worry", said the agent, "the jib is going to be removed and lowered onto the deck". "Where's this beast got to go to?" said Duff. "Gibraltar", was the answer. Three days later, the jib was removed by an even larger floating crane, and lashed down on to the deck midships with chains that were welded to the deck.

The next day they cleared harbour for Gibraltar. A radio

message delivered by Flashy told them that the tug would be ready in three weeks. "Tell them to make it four weeks", said Duff, "we need twenty-four days to get to Gib". They bunkered at Bizerta and set off for the last leg of their journey. Along the cost of Algeria, just after they had passed Oran, they were within two days steaming of Gibraltar they had a message from the Admiralty telling them that their destination had been changed from Gibraltar to Portsmouth. They decided to bunker at Tangiers yet again. Duff by this time was getting a little frustrated and told Flashy to tell Rennoldsons that the launching would have to wait. Back came the quick reply, "Don't worry, we are in the middle of a shipyard strike". Hugging the Portuguese coast they bunkered at La Curuna and were amazed to see that there were some fine new sea going salvage tugs that were stationed there. "Our new one will give them a good run for their money", said Duff.

The weather reports for the Bay of Biscay sounded unhealthy, and they decided that in the interests of safety they would hug the French coast rather than cross the Bay, but in doing so, would almost double the journey time in the Bay. This was a prudent move as they met no bad weather other than the occasional fog. On rounding Ushant they radioed their ETA only to be told that their destination had been changed yet again. This time to the Naval Base at Rosyth. This meant that they had to bunker at Southampton before they could complete the final leg. Five days later found them entering the Firth of Forth and handing over to Admiralty tugs. As soon as they dropped their charge they turned and went full speed for the Tyne. The dock strike had come to an end three days previously, so work on the new tug was continuing. Rennoldson had an empty dry dock available, so it was beneficial for the **HAINULT** to go in. They were overdue for a survey anyway. The propeller was removed as well as the tailshaft, and the stern tube was re-wooded and re-bored. At the same time her hull was scraped down and given several coats of anti-fouling paint. Her engine was stripped down and inspected. Her boiler mountings removed and machined where necessary, and a few tubes were replaced in her boilers. The surveyor remarked on the good condition of the boilers, and Taffy just grinned and said, "We look after them". Three days later she was out of dry-dock and was tied up to the fitting out basin.

Arrangements were made for the Jarrow Mayor's wife to launch the new tug, and it was hoped that **the HAINULT** could hare after her and be the first to put a line on her at her launching. All work was finished on the **HAINULT** the day before the launching and Taffy proudly brought the boilers up to a full head of steam, and warmed her engine through. The next morning, there was the platform by the side of the bows of the new tug.

"I name this ship **STELLA**, bless all who sail in her and all that are saved by her", floated across the shipyard, as the **STELLA** just glided down the slip-way gathering momentum as she went. Needless to say the **HAINULT** was the first to put a line aboard. The **HAINULT** slowly inched the **STELLA** back to the quay for examination, and the **HAINULT** tied up along side.

Duff and Taffy had already advertised for officers and crew to man the **STELLA** and one fellow Raymond George was selected as Chief Engineer and the 3rd Engineer of the **HAINULT** who had done sterling work with the **CERCUR** was promoted to become his 2nd Engineer. The mate of the **HAINULT** Bill Samuels was promoted to Master and Duff went as Master of the **STELLA**. Angel although very impressed with the galley of the **STELLA**, felt loyalty was in order, and elected to stay with Taffy on the **HAINULT**. "I've got to look after Chiefy", he said.

The contract that they had agreed to was to return ships to the United States and Canada or wherever directed, that the allies had used on a lease-lend basis. They would vary from small craft to larger vessels such as the T2 tankers and Sam boats and even war vessels. The first two vessels were to be collected from Rosyth and taken to Delaware Bay in the States. They were *HMS* **VERONICA** and *HMS* **VERA**, both World War I veterans. Those that had served on them were glad to see the back of them as the ratio of length/beam was higher than normal and in consequence pitched and rolled badly. It was decided to lash the two sisters together and both the **HAINULT** and the **STELLA** to tow at the same time. All went well till they reached Cape Hatteras (sometimes known as the graveyard of the Atlantic) where they met very high seas and winds. The **HAINULT** left the **STELLA** to the tow, while she, was attached to a bridle that had been strung aft between the two destroyers. In this way she stabilised the tow and prevented the shearing action. From Delaware Bay the **HAINULT** was instructed to sail down the Florida Straits to Key West and tow a British steamer the **EMPIRE SHOW** to the UK for breaking up on the west coast of Scotland. By the time the **HAINULT** reached Troon the **STELLA** was entering Delaware Bay with yet another V-class destroyer. Round the coast of Scotland and through the Pentland Firth where the **HAINULT** passed through force nine gales and on to Murmansk where she was to bring two large ammunition barges back to Hull. The voyage home was uneventful and the barges were safely delivered. On leaving Hull Flashy intercepted an SOS from a collier said to be grounded on the Haisborough Sands. These were considered by many as a shipping hazard. Indeed there were many wartime wrecks that bore testimony to this. Flashy asked for a position of the vessel and found that it was within ten minutes steaming.

The vessel in difficulty was easy to spot as it had slewed round. It had grounded at high tide and it would be a further three weeks before a spring tide was due. The vessel was the **WILTSHIRE** and had been drawing 18' forward and 20' aft prior to the grounding. As soon as she went aground, leads had been taken and it would found that there was only 16' of water forward. Bill Samuels the **HAINULT**'s Master decided that it would be impossible to drag her off on that tide, but there was a lot of work to be done in the next ten hours. A line was taken from the stern of the **HAINULT** to the vessel's port anchor which was gradually paid out as the **HAINULT** moved away by some 150 yards and then lowered it in the deeper channel. While this was being down, all the vessels water was pumped over the side. The **WILTSHIRE** was outward bound and had just bunkered with the best part of 700 tons of heavy fuel-oil. The bunkering tanker was recalled and all the bunkers except what was in the settling tanks were transferred. High tide was due at 22:30 and it was agreed that the **HAINULT** would begin the big pull at 22:00. Another line was brought up from the **HAINULT** and the heavy towing cable was shackled to the **WILTSHIRE**'s starboard anchor cable, and about 80 fathoms were paid out. At 22:00 an attempt to haul on the port anchor proved successful as the **WILTSHIRE** begun to swing round. This was the signal for go-go-go. The **HAINULT** steamed slowly at first towards the deep-water channel and then increased to half speed. At the same time as this was going on the **WILTSHIRE**'s engine was run up to half ahead as she gently slid off the sand bank and into deep water. The **WILTSHIRE** anchored while the **HAINULT** recovered her cables, and the bunkering tanker that had been standing-by came alongside to re-bunker her and replenish her water tanks. Three hours later the **WILTSHIRE** was on her way to Rotterdam.

The **HAINULT** then had to make the journey to Murmansk to bring two small vessels to the ship-breakers on the Clyde. These two vessels had been bombed and sunk during the war, had been raised and then sunk again as block-ships. After the war they had been raised and patched-up roughly just to make the passage to the breakers. The towing passage made very slow progress, due to the weather. At one time they were hove-to for 48 hours, just maintaining steerage way. The two vessels were delivered to the breakers, and there was a sight that really upset Taffy and Angel. **4368**, sister ship to the **HAINULT** was awaiting demolition. What a sorry state she looked. Her once proud bows partly crushed, half her deck-house was missing where she had caught a falling bomb, and she was red with rust. Having seen the **4368** they felt that they could not get away quick enough. Up to Scapa Flow to take yet another

V-class destroyer of World War I vintage that had to be taken to the Gulf of St Lawrence in Canada to Port Cartier. This meant a voyage through the North Atlantic winter gales, a formidable task. Before they set off Taffy had the destroyer fully ballasted in an attempt to stabilise the destroyer. On several occasions the destroyer took on uncontrollable shears that usually took over half an hour before they were back on course. One hundred and fifty miles from the coast of Newfoundland, the destroyer sheared so badly that the towing cable parted company. Those on board the destroyer were drenched as they valiantly pulled on the rope messenger. The messenger was received by them eventually, only by the **HAINULT** floating a messenger downwind attached to a life-belt that had been picked up by those on the destroyer using a boat-hook. After hours of heaving the **HAINULT** and her charge were on their way again. The remainder of the voyage was uneventful, and on rounding Newfoundland entered calmer waters. Homeward bound they reached the position where the towing cable had parted when Flashy intercepted an SOS from a tanker in distress.

EL MARDI

The ss **EL MARDI** was a wartime tanker of the T2 design. She had the previous day passed close to an ice-field, and had reported underwater damage. She was without power to her main engine but her Master reported her as safe, but asked for assistance. The mountainous seas meant that she was constantly buffeted. Flashy sent out a message that the **HAINULT** would be with them within the next eight hours. Round the **HAINULT** turned and they were subjected to heavy waves breaking over the stern. Three hours later the **EL MARDI** radioed to ask for any vessel nearby to render assistance as cracks were appearing between Nos. 3 and 4 tanks on the deck forward of the bridge and she was in danger of breaking up.

Flashy intercepted a message from the Coast Guard saying that one of their cutters was putting to sea in an attempt to take off the crew. By the time the **HAINULT** had the **EL MARDI** in sight the vessel had broken in two. Both sections were still afloat. The stern section was upright, although low in the water and the bow section lay abeam with the starboard rails about 4' above the water. All the ship's company had previously moved to the stern as they expected the bow section to sink. The **HAINULT** steamed gently up to the stern of the **EL MARDI** where the two Captains were able to discuss their position. Captain Gordon of the **EL MARDI** felt that they were not now in any immediate danger and that they were about 45 miles from land and about 60 miles from the nearest port of St. John (NF). The **HAINULT** was in daily contact with Duff on the **STELLA** and knew that she was about 120 miles away making a good towing speed of 6 knots with her charge. Captain Gordon of the **EL MARDI** said that he would prefer to be towed to Halifax, Nova Scotia, in preference to St. John, as Halifax had dry-docking facilities.

A messenger line was quickly passed to the stern of the **EL MARDI** and many willing hands quickly had the eyes over the bollards and the towing commenced. St John was later passed, and a day later the **STELLA** was in contact with them to say that the harbour tugs had grudgingly put to sea to take the **STELLA's** tow and allow the **STELLA** to attempt a salvage of the fore section. Duff was amazed to find the bow section still afloat and was even more surprised to find no oil slick. A radio message from the **HAINULT** informed him that not all tankers carried cargoes of oil, - this one was loaded with a cargo of wine from Spain and was bound for a winery at Boston.

Duff manoeuvred the **STELLA** to within a hundred yards of the bow and inflatable dinghy made its way to the bow section. Timing it precisely they motored in on top of a wave on to the side of the vessel, and were left high and dry as the water receded. "Didn't do the outboard motor any good", said Ray George, "reckon its completely knackered". A messenger was fired across and two of the men from the dinghy balanced themselves precariously on the side of the bows while they tried to manhandle a heavier cable from the **STELLA.** The idea was to attach it to the anchor cable. When it came to take on the main towing cable the men just tumbled down the sloping sides and into the water. However Ray George was able to haul them up one by one up the sloping side to safety, but the immersion in the water had completely sapped their strength. Duff took the unique step of nudging the bows of the **STELLA** against the damaged vessel, where his men were raised and brought back to the warmth of the **STELLA**. The **EL MARDI** bows did not go under and the Chief Engineer was still precariously balanced on the bow. So two more men were lowered over the side on to the bow. The **STELLA** gently edged alongside till her stern was level with the bows and using the after derrick, the heavy towing cable was gently lowered complete with shackle. In this way the weight of the cable was held by the **STELLA** and there was no difficulty shackling up to the anchor cable. By this time the sea was beginning to moderate, and Duff decided to pay out a length of about 500 yards. He had given instructions to one of the crew to stand by with an axe and sever the cable if he saw the **EL MARDI** go under completely. Turning the vessel's bow took them the best part of a couple of hours and they gradually worked up to a towing speed on one and half knots. It took them thirty-six hours before the coastline of Nova Scotia was sighted and it was another five hours before they were able to find the beach that had been recommended to them by the coast Guard that had a sandy bottom that was not littered with rocks. They waited for high tide and gently nudged the **EL MARDI** close to the beach and anchored.

Three hours later the sea had subsided considerably and Ray George brought an 8" hose to the near-vertical deck of the **EL MARDI**, tying himself to anything he could find, he clamped the glands of the hose to one of the cargo valves. One of the main engines of the **STELLA** was started, the screw disengaged and a main salvage pump put into operation. When Duff looked over the. side and saw the crimson liquid pouring from the tugs side into the sea, all he could say was, "Look at all that good booze going to waste". As the tide began to rise, the Chief stopped the salvage pump and brought the hose back on board. A line was thrown over and taken over the ships side rails just aft of the forecastle and a heavier line was heaved on board and made fast to a bollard. The other end was brought to the after-most part but there were no bollards in this vicinity and therefore this end was given a couple of turns round the mast and shackled together. The sea now had lost all its ferocity and was calm. All eyes on the **STELLA** were focused, waiting for the slightest movement in the **EL MARDI**. "There she goes", said one of the crew, and Duff gingerly conned the **STELLA** round till she lay at right angles to the bow section. Gently he increased revs till the wire was bar tight. She still refused to budge. Duff forever the gentlemen said, "it's now hit or bust". Warning everyone to move under cover, he lifted the emergency gates in front of the throttles, and pushed them forward till the rev counters went into the red zones. "You can't run my engines like that", said Ray, "you'll kill them. Just wait half an hour and she'll float off and you can roll her easily".

Duff decided to heed the Chief's advice, and maintained a gentle pull on the cable. Twenty minutes later those on deck were able to witness a change in shape of the **EL MARDI** as she lazily rolled on to an even keel and began riding the gentle waves. Duff was in a bit of a quandary. The towing cable that had been attached to the anchor cable had been disconnected when the **EL MARDI** had been beached. The only connection with the **EL MARDI** was over the starboard side and no way could they tow her beam on. Duff decided that it would be better to beach her once again, to effect a change over of cables. Gently nudging her bow section into the shallows once more they allowed the vessel to settle once more with the tide. The cable over the side was brought on board and stowed. The main towing cable was once again brought on deck and made fast to the anchor cable. Later that evening they celebrated their success with red wine, obviously the cook had learnt a few of Angel's tricks. Later the tide rose again and the **EL MARDI** floated off and the final leg of the tow began.

As soon as they were on their way again the **HAINULT** was radioed to tell them of their success. When the news was received, Angel started on one of his "specials". Days later the **STELLA** sailed into Halifax and "parked" the bow section in front of the after section. The **STELLA** tied up alongside the **HAINULT** and everyone trooped on to the **HAINULT** to savour Angel's special. It turned out to be steak cooked in red wine. Another "special" was a cake that was made in two parts, and the outline of it was the two halves of the **EL MARDI**, and he had iced on it in red icing! "It looks hideous", said Taffy as he helped himself to a large slice.

Subsequently the cargoes of both sections were discharged and the two halves of the vessel were taken into dry dock. The surveyors decided that a new mid-section could be built and the **EL MARDI** joined together. She was back in service four months later.

THE CRANKAY

Homeward bound from the States the **HAINULT** intercepted an SOS from the **CRANKAY**, an old steam tanker of 1926 vintage who was in difficulties. Her main circulating pump had packed up, when it had smashed beyond repair. She had been built with economy in mind, in the lean years of shipping and had no auxiliary pump to back it up, nor could her ballast pump be connected as an alternative. She had full steam to her main engine, and her auxiliaries, but because the main circulating pump was out of action, no vacuum could be raised in her main condenser. Because of this the **CRANKAY** was only able to proceed a little more than one and a half knots. She was passing through a gale with high seas and was being driven northwards towards an ice-field.

Bill Samuels plotted a course for the **CRANKAY** and Flashy radioed to say that they would be able to join her in about twelve hours. The **HAINULT** altered course and for the best part of six hours was able to run at full speed. Then she met the gale with gusts of up to 80 m.p.h. and waves 30ft or more, so that her speed had to be cut.

When the **CRANKAY** came into view she was wallowing badly in the troughs and like most tankers was loaded down to her marks, so that the waves just rolled over her. The condition of the sea prevented the **HAINULT** getting near enough to fire a line over the bows, so it was decided to attach a light line to a lifebelt and float it down-wind hoping that it would eventually reach the vessel in distress. It took another hour and half before the lifebelt neared the vessel, and by skilful manoeuvring of the **HAINULT** the lifebelt came alongside, to be plucked up by a crewman using a boat-hook. Next came across a heavier line followed by the main towing wire. While this was being hauled on board, Bill Samuels took the **HAINULT** in as near as he dared, a mere 100 yards away, but it did allow the cable to be pulled on board more easily. In the far distance they could see the first of the big growlers appearing like giant piles of sugar.

As soon as the main towing cable was made fast, Bill Samuels brought the vessel round on a southerly bearing and in to the teeth of the gale, gradually paying out the cable till there was about 600 yards between the two vessels. For a little less than ten hours they fought the elements and on reaching the edge of the storm entered calmer waters, and clear moonlight.

Now it was time for Taffy to transfer to see what could be done. An inflatable dinghy was quickly over the side and was alongside the **CRANKAY** minutes later. Taffy leapt on board, to be greeted by her Chief Engineer. Taffy was amazed when he saw the main circulating pump, never had he seen one so badly damaged, truly it was beyond repair. Taffy walked the length of the ship and engine and boiler-rooms and pondered long and hard. He then measured up pipes and fittings. The ballast pump in the engine-room could be used for pumping up or down the fore-peak tank which usually contained fresh water. The first thing he instructed the engineers to do was to fill the after-peak tank from the fore-peak tank, to preserve as much fresh water as possible. Certain 4" copper pipes were "borrowed" from the engine-room and other parts of the ship, and were fashioned to different shapes and bends. A cargo pump in the forward pump room was used to pump sea water from the forepeak tank up to deck, along the deck-lines and down to the engine-room via the new maze of pipes, to the main condenser. The ballast pump meantime, was filling the fore-peak tank with sea water. So long as the ballast pump continued to keep the fore-peak tank filled, all was well.

This meant that a partial vacuum was raised and the vessel proceeded at six knots. Once the engineers found that they could proceed at a steady speed the **HAINULT** brought in her towing cable. The crew of the **CRANKAY** were subjected to water rationing till she dropped her cargo in the UK where dry-docked and was fitted with a new pump. The **HAINULT** escorted her to the mouth of the Thames.

DORIA STAR

By this time the second tug has been launched as the **STELLA II**. The Mate Derek Brown from the **STELLA I** (as she now had to be known) was to become her Master and the 2nd Engineer of the **STELLA I** was to sail as Chief Engineer. Back to the UK went the pair of tugs to await further orders. Their arrival at Falmouth was greeted by the newsmen who were interested in the epic of the **EL MARDI**. Already, in the national papers there had been articles about the salvage of the vessel, and a full length feature on the men was envisaged. Hardly had they bunkered, than orders were through for the **HAINULT** to proceed to Middlesborough to take a 2000 ton tanker to Kiel. She has been, originally, the German **VULKANITE**, and had been captured just off Iceland in 1943 and renamed the **EMPIRE VULKAN**. She was going to Kiel for dry-docking prior to being repatriated. This was only a short run of about three days from Middlesborough, and return run was guaranteed.

As the **HAINULT** rounded Cuxhaven she was met by the Pilot cutter with two tugs in attendance. The Pilot requested that the two harbour tugs took the **EMPIRE VULKAN** along the Elbe and in to the canal. The Pilot asked that the **HAINULT** assist the vessel that had run aground. The harbour tugs took over and the **HAINULT** went full speed for the Elbe. When they reached the mouth of the Elbe they were shocked to find that the mouth of the river was littered with wrecks from the war. Some were on their beam ends and some had just sunk and many lay at strange angles where they had broken their backs. Bill Samuels remarked that the only place that he had seen such devastation before was on the Haisborough sands near the Humber. Close inshore on the western side, high and dry on the sand lay an old steamer The **DORIA STAR** that must have been at least twenty-five years old, resplendent with her woodbine funnel gaily painted out in red and white. Her engine had failed as she entered the Elbe and she had been blown ashore before any of the harbour tugs could reach her. "Why not float her off"? said Bill. "Because," said the Pilot, "she was coming in, low on bunkers, no ballast and completely empty of cargo and, worst of all she grounded at high tide at the height of a spring tide. It will be another three months before we have another spring tide as high as that one". "E'ee laddie", said Bill Samuels, "you've only got once chance now, and its going to cost you lots".

At low tide the **HAINULT** found a channel that was deep enough to accommodate her and anchored. It took a further two days before the equipment arrived, and then it was the British Army that came to the rescue. In the meantime the **HAINULT** had to put in a lot of preparatory work. At high tide the **HAINULT** took the **DORIA STAR's** anchors and laid them out as ground tackle and recovered the cables (at low tide) that had been used in the operation. She also paid out long cables up to the bows of the **DORIA STAR**, that were attached to her warping drums, in preparation for towing. The **DORIA STAR** in the meantime had been able to effect what she hoped was permanent repairs to her engine, but was unable to test the old engine as there was insufficient water at low tide to draw circulating water. As the tide receded beyond the **DORIA STAR**, three Army bulldozers edged their way across the sand. Two of the bulldozers ploughed out a channel either side of the vessel about 15' wide for the length of the vessel, about 4' deep, while the third bulldozer was scouring out a channel in front of the vessel towards the channel where the **HAINULT** lay. A couple of hours later they were joined by a giant earth scraper that moved the enormous pile of sand further inshore. The earth scraper continued moving sand till the sea was up to its axles. By this time the tide was sweeping up the new channel, and the channels both side of the **DORIA STAR** had water in them. Gradually as the tide came in, the water around the **DORIA STAR** got deeper and she began to settle as the water scoured the sand beneath.

When it was deemed high tide, the **HAINULT** winched in the tow-line till taut, the **DORIA STAR** started hauling on her windlass and her engine was gently eased up to slow ahead. Little, however was gained by this as the water level was below the level of the propeller boss. The **HAINULT** started hauling on her windlass as Bill Samuels rung down for more revolutions. Very, very slowly the **DORIA STAR** slid into the deeper water of the channel as her anchors came up, and within twenty minutes she was swinging free at her anchor in the main channel. A further half hour elapsed and the **HAINULT** had recovered and stowed the main cable in her hold.

Duff in the meantime on board the **STELLA I** received a curt telex from the Admiralty, reminding him that the **STELLA I** and the **HAINULT** were still contracted to the Admiralty for a further six months and that they felt that they, the Admiralty, were being delayed in their deliveries, due to the number of "private jobs" the HTC was doing. Taffy and Duff composed a letter between them that amounted to reminding the Admiralty that it was the duty of all those at sea to save lives and vessels. Hastily the **HAINULT** set sail for the Thames where they were to pick up an old tanker and take it round to Troon on the west coast of Scotland. Up to Scapa Flow and yet another V-class destroyer to be taken to Port Cartier in the Gulf of St. Lawrence.

In the meantime the **STELLA I** and the **STELLA II** had to tow a heavy cruiser to Key West in the Straits of Florida. There were still two more W-class destroyers and a mine-sweeper that had to be moved across the Atlantic before the contract was complete. Because of the delays that the rescues had caused the time contract would expire before they had fulfilled their contract on the number of vessels towed. Duff was able to strike a balanced deal with the Admiralty and this meant that they would just break even on the extra time and it would be based on daily hire only while towing. This meant that all three vessels would have to make a further transatlantic voyage. The **HAINULT** took the mine-sweeper in tow, and met calm sailing all the way to Key West. While the three vessels were at sea, negotiations were taking place for the salvage of the vessels that were sunk in the Elbe. At that time the Germans possessed no salvage or ocean-going tugs, however they had a few in the process of being built. They were putting most of their shipbuilding efforts into the construction for tankers and cargo vessels. The Dutch (a country who was always renowned for its powerful tugs) was still hostile to the Germans and were not interested in giving assistance.

The **HAINULT** was making her way back via the north of Scotland to the Tyne where she was going to dry-dock. As she neared the Hebrides she received an SOS from a RN mine-sweeper that was in difficulties just off Cape Wrath on the northern tip of Scotland. Flashy radioed on to say that they would be with the mine-sweeper within an hour and a half. When they did eventually spot her she looked in a sorry state, dis-masted and wallowing heavily in the swell and was well down aft. They drew alongside and with fenders between the two, lashed themselves together. The engine-room was flooded to a depth of four feet as the skylight had been shattered by a small explosion in the engine-room. A four inch hose was immediately put down there and pumping commenced. Within an hour the vessel had risen significantly to the extent that they could increase speed to five knots. Several hours later the engine-room was completely dry. Bill Samuels made sure that planks were put over the skylights and a tarpaulin was battened down. A small portable generator was placed on board, and temporary lighting was rigged up in strategic places. This enabled them at least to have an electrical supply for the galley. The Pentland Firth gave them a bit of a problem as they both bobbed about like corks. A further three days elapsed before they entered Rosyth.

THE VITTORIA

After bunkering they set off for the short leg to the Tyne and a rest while she was in dry-dock. A week or so later the **HAINULT** sailed for the Elbe, as Taffy wanted to survey some of the sunken vessels. Although Taffy had plenty of experience of using scuba diving gear, he felt it expedient to employ a full time diver for inspecting the vessels. Two of the vessels were sunk in the main channel and were a constant hazard to shipping. The German port authorities wished that these two vessels be removed before any of the others. Both were upright, though one had broken its back. Both of them had their hulls completely submerged and at high water only showed their masts and bridges.

Number one vessel, the **VITTORIA** was an old steamer with three holds that had broken its back. It was loaded with coal. As the tide receded and the vessels decks cleared of water it was observed that Nos. 1 and 3 holds were not tidal. The vessel had broken its back across No. 2 hold, however, Taffy noted, the engine-room was tidal. When Taffy went over the side with scuba gear he noted that there was a large hole in the hull of the engine-room which Taffy guessed to be about five feet by six feet, and looked remarkably like the hole made from a limpet mine explosion. Taffy had been taught to be cautious and would not venture along the section where its back was broken. The **STELLA II** in the meantime had also been in dry-dock and she and her sister were making for the Elbe. The **HAINULT** radioed them both with instructions to collect two camels each and hopper type grabs. A week later the pair of them turned into the Elbe and anchored near the wreck.

In the meantime Bill Samuels and Taffy had recruited a deep-sea diver who had inspected the vessel thoroughly, underwater. It was his confirmed opinion that the vessel was in two halves, that had parted company, however, he stated, the keel alone might be holding the two halves together. Taffy asked, if one half was lifted, would it tear itself free from the other half. The diver agreed that there was a distinct possibility of this happening. Arrangements were made for barges to be in continuous attendance for an unlimited period, into which the cargo of coal could be discharged. The following day the two **STELLAs** tied up to the **VITTORIA** as soon as her decks were clear of water. The derricks were swung over No.1 hold and the **STELLA II** working on the port side began lifting out the coal with the grabs. Slow progress was made as the water was allowed to drain from the grab before it was swung over the **STELLA II's** deck and deposited it in the barge. The **STELLA I** was unable to do any discharging as the masts and stay wires lay across the starboard side of the hatch. These were cut free and into pieces before being lowered into the starboard side barge. By the time the tide covered the decks again, the **STELLA II** had removed about ninety tons of coal. As the next tide started dropping the two **STELLAs** both started discharging the coal. Duff decided that it would be better if the **HAINULT** started pumping out the water in No.1 hold although it would flood again on each tide. On the next tide as soon as the hatch coamings were clear, the pumping commenced and long streaks of black water were found miles away that resembled oil slicks. However, the clearing of the water enabled them to place the grabs in awkward places and start the removal of coal from the corners of the hold. When the water was down to the level of coal, the **HAINULT** moved aft to start work with her grab to remove some of the cargo from No.2 hold. Between the two **STELLAs** they removed nearly two hundred tons on that tide from No.1 hold and the **HAINULT** had removed about forty tons from No.2.

As the tide rose, they knocked off, dined and slept and developed a shift pattern of six on and six off. The following tide found the **HAINULT** pumping out No.1 hold down to the level of coal before she too started heaving coal out of No.2 hold. On that tide No.1 hold was cleared bar a few tons of coal that could only be removed by shovels. As the tide rose in the early hours of the morning, slight movement of the vessel was detected, however they allowed the hold to refill in order to stabilise her. As the tide began to fall yet again, both **STELLAs** moved aft to remove as much as they could from hold No.2. This was slow progress as most of the contents of each grab was water. As the tide dropped they were able to make slightly better progress as they were able to locate the coal. While they were busy clearing the cargo in No.2 the **HAINULT** was feverishly pumping the water from No.1, till it was empty. "Didn't do the pump much good though", said Taffy.

As the tide began to rise so too did the hull. There was a grating and groaning of tired old plate being torn asunder, and the fore section was afloat. The **HAINULT** had already put a heavy line on board the bows and gently towed her to the beach, moving her in still further as the tide reached its peak.

Again the **STELLAs** were put to work emptying No.3 hold while the **HAINULT** was discharging what was left in the remainder of No.2 hold. About a week later the cargo had been completely cleared and it was found that No.3 hold was only making about 6" of water, a tide, so at least they could count on considerable buoyancy. Both the **STELLAs** put 6" hoses down into the **VITTORIA**'s engine-room, while the **HAINULT** connected hers to the after-peak tank and started pumping. The after-peak tank emptied easily and although the level of the water in the engine-room fell, it was not enough to float her. Taffy decided that she would have to have a plate put over the hold before they could pump her dry. The diver was sent down to measure the hold and Taffy's original estimate of 5' x 6' was found to be reasonably accurate. A 10mm plate was purchased ashore that measured 6' x 8' and several holes were drilled and tapped in it. At the same time a dozen or so clamping plates were made up. The diver was supplied with an abundance of nuts, washers and varying lengths of studding. The **HAINULT** gently lowered it down the vessels side into position. As he was working underwater at the time he had devised a set of signals, using a light line to the crewmen who was controlling the derrick winch. This manoeuvring of the plate took him over two hours. When it eventually came into rough position he quickly screwed a length of studding into one of the holes slipped a clamping plate on and spun a nut and washer on the studding. Having got one side of the plate partly fastened, the plate was finally positioned and clamped on to the hull. The **STELLAs** started pumping furiously and the water level dropped speedily. As this happened they detected a slight movement and the **STELLA II** transferred her hoses and the **HAINULT** started pumping No.3 hold gradually as the vessel shed her water the **VITTORIA** started rising from her watery grave where she had spent so many years.

As her tank tops cleared of water to expose slippery seaweed the diver found that there was still water pouring in. At least he could see what clamps he had to tighten to stem the flow of sea-water. He had gone down into he engine-room complete with pocketfuls of tapered plugs to push into the holes that were not needed for clamping. In carrying out these last operations he stemmed the flow to what was not much more than a heavy trickle. Those on board the stern section quickly threw a line to **the HAINULT** and a heavier cable was passed between the two, and when made fast, the **HAINULT** started chugging her way to the distant shore so that the two halves of the **VITTORIA** could lay together high on the beach. The Germans had decided that rather than tow her to the breakers yard they would break her up on the beach where she lay. Some days later on the evening spring tide the tow halves were moved even further inshore where there was no fear of them drifting.

THE OTTO ERNST

The **OTTO ERNST** was also in the deep water channel. Part of her bridge and masts were showing at high tide, and her foredeck was just awash at low tide. Her holds and engine-room were all flooded. The **OTTO ERNST** was a 4000 ton steamer that had been built in 1933 at Bremerhaven. She had three holds forward and two aft, with engine-room amidships. She had at the time of sinking been carrying a cargo of phosphates in the forward holes and grain in the after holds. Divers on entering the depths at low tide, reported finding large holes in one side of No.2 hold and another in No.5 hold. These the diver said, were large, suggesting either a hit by a torpedo or mine damage.

As there was apparently no damage to the other holds the idea of pumping Nos. 1,3 and 4 started, using the two **STELLA**s. The **HAINULT** started pumping the engine-room but soon gave up as the level dropped, while pumping was in progress. However when pumping stopped the water level rose to match the outside, thus proving it was tidal, but as there did not appear to be any holes in the hull sides there had to be holes below the engine-room and extensive damage to the tank-tops.

No.1 hold was also found to be tidal, and when the diver went down into the hold he found that most of the cargo of phosphates had been washed out. While he was down there he also found that there was a large split in the bulkhead between hold No.1 and 2 that were 12' high by 3' wide, obviously where the bulkhead had given way under the pressure of water in No.2 hold. No.2 hold was devoid of any cargo, as the action of the sea had washed it out.

The level of water in No.3 dropped quickly to the top of the cargo, as it was pumped, revealing that the phosphates, by the action of the sea-water had formed a solid mass, that was just penetrable using a chipping hammer.

When No.4 hold was inspected it was found to be a solid mass of grain that had rotted and fused together, though it was quite porous. It was considered that its removal would not be too much of a problem.

One problem that did reveal itself was that if No.4 hold was cleared then the bulkhead between it and No.5 might collapse. No.5 hold's damage had to be rectified first. The other problem that was considered was that if hold Nos. 2, 4 and 5 were sealed and discharged the buoyancy gained might cause the vessel to break her back.

The plan of action dictated that the hole in No.5 hold was sealed, and a large plate 10mm thick was lowered down the vessel's side into rough position at low tide. The first two clamps were applied while the two **STELLA**s and the **HAINULT** pumped for all they were worth. With the plate covering most of the hole in the ships side the plate was jogged into its final position where the remainder of the clamps were applied and tightened up. This work took three tides before it was decided that the hold was somewhere near water-tight. The hold was allowed to flood at each high tide.

The following days found the two **STELLA**s again using the grabs to discharge No.4 hold and maintaining an equal water level between 4 and 5 holds, to prevent the bulkhead giving way. It took the three tugs a whole week before No.4 hold was empty. As the days progressed it did get easier as, as soon as the tide uncovered the hatch coamings pumping commenced immediately, and it became increasingly easy to see the cargo that had to be recovered.

The same problems of a collapsing bulkhead could occur between No.3 and 2 holds, so that it was essential that No.2 hold was patched and part pumped before No.3 hold was discharged. The hole was plated in the same way and the hold was pumped down low. This took a further four tides work to finally position the plate. When the hold was pumped down below the level of the plate there was still an enormous amount of water pouring in through the gaps between hull and plate. These gaps were finally closed up by hammering in numerous wooden wedges. These stemmed the flow of water till it was down to a heavy trickle.

This final closing up took a further two tides, and after closing the hold was allowed to flood again with the tide.

Now the serious business of emptying No.3 hold could begin. The River Authorities had warned the HAINULT TOWAGE COMPANY that they would be contravening regulations by dumping the phosphates over the side. They further stated that the cost of hiring barges/lighters for removal of the phosphates was the responsibility of the salvers, however they would be prepared to pay 50% of the hire charges, and ensure the proper disposal of the phosphates.

On each tide the crew of the three vessels worked feverishly with pickaxes breaking up the fused mass. As it was broken up, it was shovelled into the grabs, and transferred to the barges. From the time that the water receded to the time it flowed back into the hold over the hatch coamings was less than four hours working time. In the first few days half an hour was spent pumping the water and three and a half was spent discharging the phosphates. As the days progressed and the level of cargo fell, more time was spent in pumping and less time in discharge, and they did lose a whole weeks discharge due to the weather. The vessel was lashed by high waves which, even at low tide sloshed up so much water that it prevented them working. When the weather did eventually moderate it was decided to try using the grabs to try and claw up the phosphate, and when this was attempted it met with little success. Then Taffy suggested that the grabs should have teeth welded on to the clawing faces. This modification was carried out on one grab, between tides, and when put into use met with considerable success, as it removed far more of the cargo. The advantage of using the new-styled grab was that the removal of the phosphates could continue even when the hold was flooded. One of the other grabs was adapted in the same way and the remainder of the cargo was quickly removed.

On each tide the water still had to be pumped from the hold. As the working level dropped in No.3 hold, No.2 hold and the engine-room had to also be pumped to prevent bulkhead collapse, and the remaining cargo had to be viewed. With the last of the cargo removed it meant that the vessel was reasonably water-tight with the exception of the engine-room.

A spring tide was due the following week and it was decided to suspend operations till then. The whole of the ships company of each vessel had been working long hours over many weeks (with the exception of the bad weather break) and needed a rest. On the due date all three vessels were alongside the **OTTO ERNST** at high tide, and as soon as No.1 hatch coaming was exposed the **HAINULT** and the two **STELLA**s started pumping. As the tide dropped a further half-metre the **STELLA II** started on No.2. Another hour was to elapse before the **STELLA I** moved from No.1 hold to No.3 hold and started work there. By the time the water level in No.1 hold was down to the tween-decks, the two **STELLA**s upped their hoses to start work on holds No.4 and 5. They had been pumping for about an hour when those on the **HAINULT** shouted back to them that the **OTTO ERNST** had moved slightly by the bow. They had already laid out ground tackle to prevent her swinging very far. They only had about an hour left before the tide would cover the aft section. They were not to be disappointed, within the half hour the after section began to become buoyant. This meant that for the first time they could continue pumping the vessel at high tide. The vessel slowly rose out of the water till the weed and barnacle encrusted hull was three feet above the surface of the water.

The **HAINULT** quickly shipped her hoses, put a heavy line aboard the **OTTO ERNST**, those on board her let go of the ground tackle and she was gently edged from the deep water channel towards the shallows. It was the responsibility of the **HAINULT** to hold the **OTTO ERNST** against the incoming tide while the two **STELLA**s continued pumping the vessel. The vessel was brought so near to the beach that the **STELLA**s had very little water beneath them, and as soon as the vessel was beached they had to beat a hasty retreat, so that they too were not beached. The **HAINULT** paid out a lot of cable so that she could stay afloat during the fall of the tide. At low tide the **OTTO ERNST** lay on the beach high and dry, and it was possible for work to commence on the engine-room. On examination it was found that the tank tops were ruptured through corrosion in two places in the engine-room and one in the boiler-room, and both of these areas drained themselves at low tide. 10mm plates were cut to size and welded over the holes. Even this work took a total of eight tides. By the time this was achieved very little water was entering the vessel on the tides. When all the openings were closed up, the **OTTO ERNST** was towed closer inshore on a spring tide and she was secured to shore-side bollards.

One evening while the **HAINULT** was in Bremerhaven one of the crew was heard to say to another, "I reckon that bloke Angel's queer, have you noticed how he never goes ashore, and often calls us dears. He's a bloody good cook, but I think he's a poof". The other crewman said, "He seems quite close to the Chief Engineer, and he's the only one who can get away with calling him Chiefy. When I tried it I got my head bawled off. All Angel gets is don't call me Chiefy, I reckon they're both queers". Little did they know that their conversation was being overhead by the Bosun, who said, "For a pound or a pinch I'd tear the skin off both of you, you twisted sods. If you fell over the side in Arctic waters the Chief would go over the side for you and would make sure that you were all right. I wasn't on this vessel during the war, but Captain Duff of the **STELLA I** told me the whole story of the Chief saving Angel, and later on, Angel's attempt at saving the Chief. He even lost his balls in the attempt". "You're joking about his balls though". "No I'm not", said the Bosun, "So you will see that there will always be a strong loyalty between the two. And neither is bent".

ZELTO AND ZONDO

The German authorities considered that the main deep-water channels of the Elbe were now free of all obstructions, and that work could now commence in the lifting of the wrecks in some of the lesser channels. Two of the vessels were the **ZELTO** and the **ZONDO**, coasters of 1500tons each, which only ever exposed their decks when there was a neap tide. Both of them had been built in Sweden in 1934 and 1935 respectively. They were both clearly marked with buoys since they had sunk and there had been no movement in either vessel. The **ZELTO**, they decided, should be lifted first as she was farthest from the shore.

The diver was sent down to inspect the **ZELTO** at low tide and later reported that the vessel did not appear to be holed in any way, and that he did not think that it would be difficult to lift her from the bottom using camels. Taffy asked the diver what cargo was in her, and he replied that No.1 hold contained two Panzer tanks, in No.2 there was an abundance of packing crates, which were difficult to inspect as the wood had rotted and was impeding movement around the hold. No.3 hold held another two tanks. Taffy and Duff discussed the vessel at length and decided that on the removal of as much cargo as possible before attempting to lift her.

Many hours were spent in positioning the two **STELLA**s so that their derricks were plumbed over the vessel's No.1 hold. While they were doing this the diver was down in the hold shackling chains to the first tank, fortunately which had four lifting brackets mounted on each of the upper-works. Once the diver had located the brackets the shackling up was easy. However on several occasions the diver slid over the sloping sides due to the growth of seaweed. This seemingly small job took the diver six hours to complete, and when he climbed back on board the **HAINAULT** he was utterly exhausted. The following day he was down there again when the two **STELLA**s lowered their cables from their derricks down to the diver, whose job it was to shackle the lifting cables to the lifting eye. When the cables were lowered they did not come down immediately over the centre of the tank, and he realised that as soon as the tank started rising that it would career to the side. He therefore decided to come up for safety's sake. As he surfaced the two **STELLA**s started their winches and very, very slowly the cables started coming up. However the winches groaned so much and the tugs started heeling a bit that the winch operators both stopped them. The diver once more went down and found that one side of the tank was trapped under the hatch coaming. Neither vessel had the ability to move sideways, so the tanks was lowered and the **HAINAULT** pushed the **STELLA II** over the short distance and then pushed her sister into position. The winches were put into operation again and slowly the tank came to the surface. She still looked an evil beast, even with all the seaweed on her which partly disguised her. The **HAINAULT** already had a barge standing by and as soon as the tank was high enough the **HAINAULT** edged the barge under the tank. The barge sank lower and lower into the water till Duff thought that they might have to stop lowering. However the barge took the weight when there was only four inches of free-board. "Good job it was dead calm", said Taffy.

One of the crew disconnected the lifting cables from the top of the tank. The **HAINAULT** set off for Cuxhaven with the barge in tow. Flashy radioed ahead to tell the authorities that they were on their way with the barge, and that the barge had a very small free-board. No sooner had they left the scene they were escorted by a Pilot cutter shooed away, using its hooter, any vessel that ventured near.

The following day the diver was down again, placing the chains on the second tank. The lifting eye, this time was draped over the gun turret, and again the diver came up utterly exhausted, and it was decided to suspend operations for the day. Early next morning when the tide was at it highest, the **STELLA I** lowered her derrick cable over the sunken vessel and down went the diver. This time the derrick cable was within inches of the lifting eye. Having found the correct position, the **STELLA II** edged her way in and lowered her cable down as well, so that her lifting cable could be shackled up as well. The diver was taking no chances and come up to tell them that all was well and to start hauling. No problems were encountered this time and several hours later another tank was on its way to Cuxhaven. When the first tank had arrived at Cuxhaven an engineer had removed a plate from the bottom of the tank and allowed the water to run out, but because the aperture was so small it took several hours before the tank was drained. The engineer suggested that each tank was drained before it was put into the barge for transit just to reduce its weight.

The two **STELLA**s successfully raised the other two tanks and as each was swung over the barge Taffy jumped on to the barge, removed the plate and allowed the water to drain into the barge. "No way are we going to have a tank dangling on the end of a wire while we wait for the water to run out", said Taffy. After each tank had been lifted on to the quay, the **HAINAULT** pumped out the barge before bring it back to the lifting site. There was a gap of four days between lifting out the third and fourth tanks as the weather became stormy and became unsafe for the tugs to stay on the scene.

When the last tank was safely ashore there remained the emptying of No.3 hold of its crates. The only way to do this said Taffy and Duff together, was to use the grabs and hope that they could get hold of the loads. The next two days were spent rigging the grabs, and at first light the following day the grabs were lowered into the hold. The first load on its way up contained a lot of crashed wood, but among the debris was a large engine. Successive lifts over the next few days proved fruitful and on the fourth day the diver went down before clearance commenced. His sole purpose was to see how much cargo was left in the hold. On reaching the surface he reported that there remained four engines and other bits of equipment. The consensus of opinion was that there was little more that could be done to lighten the vessel and the easiest option was to wait two weeks till the next neap tide in the hope that the hold could be pumped.

Two weeks seemed a long time in coming. After two weeks of calm weather, one morning a storm blew up and the three tugs had to seek refuge inshore. Duff said, "If it comes up slow it takes a long time to die down. If it comes up quick it goes down quick". For two days it raged and then went quiet and the skies cleared to brilliant sunshine, but still the sea was running high, and Duff thought that they might have to wait for yet another neap tide. The following day it dawned with a clear sky, and about 8.30 the hatch tops cleared of water and they started pumping all holds. Low water was due to last for only about forty-five minutes. So the two **STELLA**s had their four salvage pumps running at full speed pumping out Nos. 1 & 3 holds, while the **HAINAULT** pumped the engine-room. The tide started rising and stated to cover the decks before the **ZELTO** started rising and even some of the waves sloshed over the coamings into the holds.

The water level in the engine-room dropped drastically and as such gave positive buoyancy. Having lowered the engine-room level the **HAINAULT** transferred her attention to No.2 hold and started pumping for all she was worth.

The levels in Nos. 1 & 3 holds were by this time about four inches below the deck level and were continuing to fall slowly, but the sheer weight of water in No.2 was keeping her low in the water. As the water level in No.2 began to drop the **ZELTO** began to rise clear of the water so that her decks were now clear of the sea. It was then that they realised that the tide that for at least forty-five minutes had been working against them it was now working for them and moving the vessel inshore. Duff now felt that the **ZELTO** had little chance of sinking, so the **HAINAULT** started towing her while the two **STELLA**s continued pumping. A further three hours found the **ZELTO** grounding on one of the many sandbanks that littered the River Elbe. This was just what they wanted to complete the pumping, but there was only one problem. The two **STELLA**s were not able to do any more pumping, as their draught would not allow them to come alongside.. The **HAINAULT** continued pumping the holds and engine-room in turn, for the next six hours till the **ZELTO** was afloat again. Bill Samuels then brought the vessel into deeper water again so that the other two tugs could finish the pumping of the holds. By this time the next high tide was imminent. The **HAINAULT** had beached the **ZELTO** up on the beach with the other wrecks.

The **ZONDO** was considered a far more formidable task. Her after mast only was visible at low tide, and when the diver had inspected her he reported that she lay with about a 20degree list to starboard, and had suffered severe damage to the bows and collision bulkhead, as if she had hit a mine. Her foremast was broken and draped over No.2 hold. When the diver came up from his second inspection, he announced that No.1 hold contained two crates, No.2 a Panza tank and an armoured personnel carrier, while No.3 contained two more tanks. All this meant that the removal of the tanks would be extremely difficult due to the list of the vessel. The armoured personnel carrier lay against the tank and was wedging it against starboard side. There would be similar problems with the other two tanks. The **HAINAULT** positioned herself so that her grab was plumbed over No.1 hold and start clawing out whatever she could and depositing it in a waiting barge. Out came a multitude of small engines and a couple of machine tools. Meanwhile the diver was attaching cables to the foremast so that too could join the scrap metal in the barge. This operation alone took a day. When the mast had been cleared the diver's next job was to attach cables to the armoured personnel carrier. This was particularly difficult as there were no lifting brackets, and he eventually shackled the cables to the vehicle's axles, this took him a further two days. By this time No.1 hold was clear.

The following day found the **STELLA II** lowering her derrick cable to the diver to begin the lift of the carrier. No sooner had the cable started coming up than the tug started heeling over, and all thought the carrier was trapped under the deck-head. The diver though exhausted went down again only to find that the lift was free of obstacles. They had underestimated the weight of the carrier. The following morning the **STELLA I** lowered her cable alongside the other which too was shackled up and the carrier was brought to the surface.

By the time it was in the barge, the weather began to break from the west, and the task of towing the barge with only four inches of free-board did not appeal to Bill Samuels as he surveyed the rising sea. Knowing that to tow it to Cuxhaven would be to fight the weather at its worst, He took the barge close to the shore and anchored. His idea was that if the barge did founder, at least he would be able to pump it dry at low tide. This forethought was a worthwhile one as shortly after, the barge disappeared from view as it sank like a stone. For days the storm raged, but the **HAINAULT** was safe as she was tethered aft by the sunken barge and forward by her own anchors and because the seas were running so high she never grounded. When the storm did eventually blow herself out, she had to wait for the following low tide before she could beach herself alongside the barge. Now she could pump out the barge. While doing this Bill Samuels took the unprecedented step of putting a hose inside the carrier and pumping it dry. The barge rode on the gentle swell of the rising tide as it was towed to Cuxhaven.

Four difficult days elapsed before the tank was lowered into a barge, It had "snagged" on the deck-head twice before a successful lift was made.

Now the serious business of lifting the **ZONDO** could commence. A cable was passed between the two **STELLA**s and the loop between them was lowered to the sea-bed behind the vessel. It was gradually inched forward till it was under the rudder and stern frame. The two tugs powered on in an attempt the drag the cable as far forward as possible.

Alas, they were only able to pull it along by some six feet. This meant that they had to use a see-saw method of moving the cable, and instead of moving parallel to the **ZONDO** they now lay at right angles to her. The **STELLA II** paid out more cable and the **STELLA I** started steaming off at right angles while the **STELLA II** would move forward. This operation was repeated but the **STELLA I** would now move forward. This went on all day till they had moved the cable a quarter of the vessel's length.

The following day, a heavy chain, resembling a medium anchor chain was brought up from the **STELLA I**'s hold and shackled to the end of the cable, and this was hauled by the other tug till it lay beneath the **ZONDO** with the ends of the chain extending either side of the vessel. They were cautious to the extent that they knew that subsequent tides would move silt and sand along the river which would then cover the chain and to remedy this the ends of the chain were buoyed. The whole process was repeated from the bow end of the vessel and it was many days before the chains were positioned and buoyed.

The camels were towed out by the **HAINAULT** to the site and positioned close to the ends of the chain and allowed to flood. In the meantime another diver had been recruited, and both of them descended to shackle up each of the camels to the chains. For a full six hours both of them toiled in the depths to achieve the result, being assisted from the surface by the **HAINAULT** gently taking the weight of the chain. Both the divers came up utterly exhausted and from then onwards the pair of them set themselves the target of making one connection a day. By the fourth day it was reckoned that everything was ready for lifting and a dawn start the following day was envisaged. As each camel had a lifting capacity of 500tons, not much trouble was envisaged.

The two **STELLA**s positioned themselves either side, so the their hoses could be attached to the camels on that side, and their compressors were started so that air was now being pumped into the camels to force out the water. Within a couple of hours, bubbles were seen rising from the camels' positions indicating that the water was emptying. The next thing that was noticed was that the mast of the **ZONDO** started heeling over, indicating that she was beginning to list still further, as she began to lift.

There was an immediate danger of capsizing, so the air supply to the port side was stopped and continued on the starboard side. This had the effect of bringing the vessel to a lesser degree of list. As the vessel continued to rise, she started to list the opposite way by a few degrees. All those on the scene were aware that the vessel could now roll off the chains, but it was imperative that she was brought closer to the surface. Air was still being force into the starboard camels, and it was decided to pump a small quantity of air into the port camels to bring her yet again on an even keel. As this was being done the top of the vessels bridge broke the surface. The inflatable dinghy was put over the side and two of the crew from the **HAINAULT** took a line from the **HAINAULT** and passed it through two portholes on the bridge and a heavier cable was passed over to replace the line, and the two ends shackled together. Bill Samuels, on the **HAINAULT** took the dangerous step and came alongside the upper works with a heavy towing cable suspended from it out-slung derrick. This was manoeuvred in from the waiting men and then shackled to the existing shackle. The **ZONDO** could now be moved into shallower water. The **HAINAULT** very slowly inched her way forward till the vessel grounded. When this happened she anchored and the camels were allowed to flood.

At the next low tide the hatches were visible but still awash. They now had a choice, they could wait for the next neap tide when she would surely be clear of water, or the chains should be shortened-up. By this time the vessel was lying on an even keel. Taking option one meant a wait of a ten days providing the weather held good. The latter option held the best possibilities . The divers went down and they found that the shortening-up of the chains could easily be done with the two **STELLA**s taking the weight of the chains.

In the course of two days all was ready. Each chain had been shortened-up by some ten feet, and this in turn meant that on the next lift the deck should be clear to start pumping out the water.

When the bubbles started emitting from the camels the next time, the **ZONDO** came alive. Her bridge came up and this was followed by her bows. Within another ten minutes her decks were clear and she had a few inches of free-board. As soon as the vessel started rising, both **STELLA**s hooted and Bill Samuels started inching the **HAINAULT** forward till the **ZONDO** grounded again. As the tide rose both **STELLA**s moved moved very slowly toward the **ZONDO**, as they were concerned about their propellers coming into contact with the camels that were still under water and not yet visible. Their salvage hoses were lowered into the holds and pumping started. As the vessel rose further out of the water she was brought further into the shallows by the **HAINAULT** as the other two cast off for deeper water.

Throughout the fall of the tide the **HAINAULT** pumped each hold in turn as well as the engine-room, but No .1 hold still presented a problem with the collapsed bulkheads. As the next high tide rose, the **ZONDO** floated freely, though well down by the head, and the **HAINAULT** her into deeper water where the other two tugs could complete the emptying of holds Nos 2 & 3. When this was achieved she was moved close inshore while the **STELLA**s went to recover the camels.

At low tide the **ZONDO** lay in about six feet of water, but this was low enough for baulks of timber to be placed in the holed bulkheads and wedged up. As the tide rose the **HAINAULT** started pumping No.1 hold and the ingress of water so small that the ZONDO was pushed up on to the beach to join the others in the "graveyard". By this time some of them were beginning to change shape as the breakers were well into the job of demolition.

THE HEINTZ

There remained one more vessel to raise, she was in one of the shallow channels and had sunk 4' into the mud. Her name was not known even though she was buoyed, however she lay in a position that was outside the buoyed channels and therefore did not present a hazard. The **STELLA**s anchored close to her and a diver was sent down to locate her and buoy her fore and aft. The inspection of the vessel by the diver on the following day, revealed that she was a small coaster of approximately 300 tons. What appeared to be ingots of iron were in both holds, and she appeared to have broken in three pieces. She had engine-room aft, bridge amidships and she appeared to have broken across No.2 hold and just forward of the bridge. Removal of the ingots from the holds would be slow but not too difficult with the grabs, but the raising of the vessel to the surface would present some difficulties.

The two **STELLA**s positioned themselves so that the grabs could be lowered into the holds. As they came up, vast quantities of water drained away from the grabs and each grabfull rendered a quantity of only about ten or so ingots, and were deposited into waiting barges. For days the grabs and went down and up till the only thing that they contained was water. Down went the diver to report the cargo position, and on reaching the surface reported that the centre of the cargo in each hold was clear but that the ingots were piled high either side of the hold. A grab was lowered into No.1 hold and the diver followed it down. One by one he lifted up the 10kg ingots and placed them in the grab. In the space of three hours he had filled the grab, and he came up exhausted. That afternoon two of the **STELLA I's** crew donned scuba sets and new-fangled commodities known as wet suits, and descended to the depths of the same hold. They found that their movements were restricted less than the diver's and that within the hour the grab was full and could be brought to the surface. By this time their air supply was down to a minimum so it was time for them to return to the surface anyway. Four more of the crew, two of each hold went down for the next few hours and worked solidly to remove the cargo, coming up only to replenish their cylinders. The clearance of the cargo took them the best part of a fortnight.

Duff and Taffy decided to take a bit of a gamble in the lifting operation. They had thought of using the camels for lifting in the conventional way, but to attempt to pass cables under the hull and then replace them with heavy chains might break up the vessel still further. A short heavy cable was lowered by the **HAINULT** and shackled to the anchor chain up in the bows. A camel was lowered as it flooded to a depth of about 6ft above the bow and shackled on to the cable. This part was easy. What did take a further three days was the lowering of the cable down to the level of the small bridge. Below the bridge were four cabins and a small room presumably a dining area. The diver entered the cabins and attempted to smash the glass in the portlight, without success. After feverish activity with a hammer and chisel he was able to get the portlight open, and then he had to repeat the operation on the other side of the vessel.

The following morning found him entering the cabin again, where someone outside with a scuba set passed him a small line which he pulled through the doors of the dining area and out through the portlight on the other side. As soon as it was through the second portlight it was attached to a cable and the line was hauled by the **HAINULT**. She continued to haul after a heavier line had been shackled on. This was slow work as the shackle often snagged on doorways and portlights, and to free it meant a trip down for the diver who loosened it with a crowbar. Eventually a heavy duty chain was hauled down that was already attached to one of the camels. As the camel flooded it was allowed to sink to the level of the bridge while the chain was continually hauled. The second camel was shackled up to the free side of the chain to complete the purchase.

There was not much on the stern section that could be

used to gain purchase. The bollards were small and looked as if they would part company with the deck, and a lot of the capstan lay in pieces on the deck. The diver decided that the only good purchase point was the main engine itself, and the fourth camel was lowered with a short chain dangling below it. This was easily attached to one of the side frames of the engine by means of shackling.

The plan of operation was to bring the vessel to the surface in several stages, beaching it each time and shortening up the cables and chains and bringing it in still further. By this time it had been established that the vessel was the **HEINTZ**, a 300 ton coaster built at Keil in 1924.

Days later the two **STELLAs** coupled up their air hoses to the camels and the water in them gently blown out. The first part of the **HEINTZ** that was exposed was the funnel or what was left of it. This was quickly followed by the top of the bridge, and what alarmed them all was the sudden appearance of the surface of the camel that had been attached to the bow section. The **HAINULT** quickly started towing the camel to the shallows where the fore section lay with her after part dragging on the bottom. As the tide rose still further she was allowed to settle on the bottom.

Meanwhile the **STELLAs** were moving the mid and stern section closer to the shore. The movement, fortunately, did not cause them to part company and their progress towards the shore on that tide was in the order of 50 yards before she settled on the bottom. As the tide began to rise again, the water from the three camels was completely evacuated and the vessel made a further progress of about 90 yards. They knew that the progress on the following tide would be minimal and decided that it was necessary to shorten up the chains. At low tide the camels dropped, the chain hauled through on one side and shortened up on the other. The same was done with the chain attached to the engine.

By this time the whole of the bridge and the poop deck were exposed, and as the tide rose, the **HEINTZ** lifted and was towed further into the shallows. All of a sudden she came to a halt and even when the two **STELLA**s increased power she refused to move.

The echo sounders on both tugs indicated that there should be at least 6ft under the **HEINTZ**. An hour later the vessel was clear of the underwater obstruction and was brought in a further 150 yards. This would mean that at low tide she would be completely exposed. The underwater obstruction had in the meantime been buoyed.

On investigation at low tide, the **HEINTZ** lay in about three feet of water and as she was now laying on an even keel the two sections had closed up to leave only a small gap. Arrangements were made for the following tide, that braces would be welded along the deck to prevent the two halves parting company, and attempt to plug the holes and splits. As soon as the decks were clear, the welding cables were run over from the **HAINULT**'s portable welding generator, and the braces were welded in position. As the water level dropped in the hold, the engine-room was pumped dry and plates were welded over the splits in her sides. All this welding was difficult work, as there was a lot of sea-weed and marine growth that had to be removed before a welding could be commenced.

As the tide rose the **HAINULT** started pumping out the hold and although the ingress of water was heavy, the **HEINTZ** water level did not appear to increase, and hour by hour she was brought closer inshore. At low tide (which happened to be a neap tide) she was high and dry. The hold drained out and wooden planks were put over the holes and stuffed with lumps of sacking filled with sawdust. As the tide rose the sawdust swelled and filled the holes so that she floated freely. At high tide the **HAINULT** pulled her high into the graveyard.

There still remained the final salvage of the fore section. The **STELLA**s attached their main towing cables to the camel and on the incoming tide pushed the throttles of both vessels right up to the maximum in the green. The foam was gushing forth behind each vessel and for the next two hours the screws strained away to the extent that they had moved the bow section some 150 yards. They stopped when the tide reached its fullest. The **HAINULT** was by this time recovering the camels from the aft sections.

A cable was lowered between the two **STELLA**s and lowered beneath the bow. For two days they see-sawed the cable till it lay about 8' from the broken part of the section. At low tide the cable was attached to a camel and hauled alongside the starboard side of the hull. A second camel was lowered into position on the port side and shackled up. The camel on the bow was shortened up still further on the following tide. As the tide began to rise, so too did the **HEINTZ**, and they were able to bring her the remaining 100 or so yards where they knew she would be high and dry at low tide.

The two after camels could be shortened up by only 3ft, and the one on the bow was now removed completely. The **HEINTZ** anchor was lowered into the water and a cable from the **HAINAULT's** derrick lifted it up while Taffy cut through it with a flame cutter. The anchor was then lifted up and placed in a waiting barge. The whole of the anchor chain was lifted out of the chain locker and put in the barge. The next operation was to pump out the fore peak tank and the chain locker. There was not a great deal of water in these compartments but it was essential that every bit of buoyancy in the bows was gained. As the tide rose the **HEINTZ** stood well out of the water and as it rose to its fullest extent she was brought by the **HAINULT** to her final resting place.

As far as the German authorities were concerned the HAINULT TOWING COMPAY had fulfilled their obligations. Duff and Taffy knew that there was still yet another underwater obstruction. When the Authorities were told about the obstruction they said that they no knowledge of any vessel sinking in that position. They agreed that the obstruction should be removed at their expense and the HAINULT TOWING COMPANY would be entitled to half of any salvage value.

The diver was sent down and quickly reported that the vessel that lay underwater was in fact a large barge loaded to the top of the hatch coamings with small coal, possibly anthracite. Part of the tarpaulin and many of the hatch-boards were still in position. This fact alone required the diver to go down a couple more times to clear them. By this time the HAINULT TOWING COMPANY was well versed in the removal of coal from underwater vessels, and in the space of two days all the cargo had been removed. The barge, **XXXII**, "Is in good condition", said the diver, "and looks as if it has only been down there for a few months".

On the bow of the barge was a very stout pair of bitts which provided it's means of towage. It was hoped that the two **STELLA**s could drag the barge far enough to beach her, using the tides action to assist in the beaching. Again the sterns of the tugs frothed as the screws bit deep and, inch by inch, yard by yard they moved forward. They were fortunate enough to pull the barge the extra 150 yards, and the **HAINULT** beached herself within yards of the sunken vessel. When the tide dropped to its lowest ebb, the coamings were just clear of the water and the **HAINULT** was able to start her salvage pumps and pump out some of the water. The barge began to float when there was only a few inches of freeboard. In fact her deck was still awash. Gradually she rose out of the water, where the **HAINULT** brought her out into deeper water where the **STELLA**s could bring their pumps to bear. By the time the tide was at its height the barge **XXXII** was all but dry, and the **HAINULT** towed her to Cuxhaven where she was handed over to the Authorities.

THE RIALTO

The **RIALTO** was a 11000ton motor vessel built in 1936 at Glasgow. She had been built as a cargo liner and had been operated as the **BERWICK CASTLE** for four years. As war broke out, she was converted to a troop carrier and renamed the **EMPIRE TOPER**, and was responsible for bringing many of the troops to the south Mediterranean landings. She had continued in the role of troop carrier till late 1946 when she was sold to Cruise Italiano Inc. and renamed **RIALTO**. She was extensively modernised and given a new fore-section that increased her length by some 50'. Her main engines had been given a very extensive overhaul, and she started her first mission as a cruise liner in May 1947 and for a year began her cruises at Lisbon with stop-overs at Tangiers, Tunis, Sardinia, Malta and the Greek Islands. She usually carried about 150 1st Class and 250 2nd Class passengers, added to this there was an additional 250 officers and crew.

One morning on the 4-8 watch Luigi Romanulli, the 2nd Engineer, spotted oil trickling down the front of one of the four 10 cylinder diesel generators. The din in the generator room was terrific as three of the four generators were running. This was because the vessel was equipped with an all-electric galley, and the galley crew had started preparations for breakfast for over 600 people. Luigi quickly noted that there were leaks on two of the fuel valves and went to the engine-room stores for the appropriate spanner. He quickly slid down the handrails of the ladder from the stores to the main deck of the engine-room and from there to the generator room. There was a further ladder that he had to negotiate up to the level of the cylinder heads. Above this was a runged platform that ran along by the side of the cylinder heads. The leaks had increased considerably in the time that had elapsed from the first viewing, and was now beginning to spray out. Knowing that he would be blinded by the spray if he went closer, he rushed back to the engine-room stores for a pair of goggles. As he retraced his steps to the generator he noticed that the fuel oil was spraying on to the exhaust pipe. The exhaust pipe was heavily lagged along its whole length except the flanges and about 2" either side of the flanges. The diesel oil was spraying directly on to this area, where it was immediately turning into thick smoke and acrid fumes. He started tightening up the nuts to the fuel valves but started panicking and in so doing badly twisted the fuel pipe and fractured it. Diesel fuel oil under pressure poured out and added to the fumes already present.

Panicking still further, instead of starting up the fourth generator and putting it on the distribution board and taking the failing generator off, he shut down the failing generator just as the exhaust pipe ignited the fuel oil. The flames, only a few inches high at first, were enough to ignite the fuel oil that lay on top of the cylinder heads. Luigi backed off as the flames spread along the whole row of cylinder heads within seconds. Within a minute, the whole of the engine-room and generator room was plunged into darkness except for the emergency lighting, as the distribution board became overloaded and the contact breakers tripped out. The flames licked their way up the leaky fuel-lines that fed the other generators.

The smoke billowed in the generator room to the extent that it was also billowing out of the ventilators on deck. Being an older vessel she had not been fitted with an automatic sprinkler system. One of the other problems that arose from being an older vessel was that the main engines had independent fuel oil pumps, and when the contact breakers had tripped out her main engines had ground to a half. The fire was escalating at an enormous rate. The only pump that could now be put into service was the auxiliary fire pump situated aft, deep down in the steering compartment. By the time this was started the whole of the generator room was ablaze and the burning paint and oil, both lubricating oil and fuel oil created acrid fumes that began to fill the engine-room.

These fumes drifted upward and through the engine-room skylights so that passengers started panicking as the thick palls of smoke curled through. Many of the passengers started congregating on the boat-deck expecting the ship to be abandoned at any minute. The engineers had shut all doors to the engine-room in an attempt to stem the spread of fire, but hoses had to be connected to the fire main in the engineers accommodation. When the connections had been made, one of the engineers opened the door from the engineers' bathroom to the engine-room. The smoke was so thick and heavy that to progress an entry was impossible.

Having given up on the attempt from this entry, there were two other alternative entrances. One was via the shaft tunnels from the steering flat which would have been extremely difficult to bring hoses down. The other entrance was via the fridge engine room, one deck below the main passenger deck. The engineers quickly coupled up hoses to the hydrants and brought them to the door in the fridge room. When the door was opened, flames shot out engulfing the Chief Engineer who immediately fell down screaming. The 3rd Engineer who had been standing to one side with the fire hose directed the stream of water through the door, and he and the 2nd Engineer started moving slowly forward into the engine-room.

All the generators by this time had stopped, but the noise in the engine-room was terrible as tins of paint and cleaning materials were exploding with regularity. One of the main engine settling fuel tanks had ruptured due to the heat and the fuel oil was pouring from it down to the floor of the engine-room only to fuel the flames still further.

From the outside of the ship it could be seen that the hull in the vicinity of the generator room and the forward part of the engine-room, was glowing red from the heat, and clouds of steam were rising from the water line. By this time the Captain decided that although he knew the ship would not sink, he was unsure how far the fire would spread. the order went out to abandon ship, and the lifeboats were swung out, and passengers rapidly filled them.

As the lifeboats began to fill, they were lowered by the crew as soon as an officer was in place in each. There were loud screams as the boats were lowered past the glowing hull and the paint began to bubble and smoke on the side of the lifeboats.

Many of the occupants decided that they would be safer in the water and jumped over the sides, instead of crouching down in the lifeboats. The remaining occupants hastily moved over to the outboard sides and so heavy did they become that they capsized, and four lifeboats were lost in this way. The Captain, as soon as the fire had started in the generator room had radioed for assistance, and several cargo ships and two tankers had changed course to assist in the rescue and pick up of survivors.

The rescue ships slowly circled the lifeboats, and one by one, the passengers were brought on board. As each vessel filled itself with the survivors they left the scene. One of the tankers that arrived after all the survivors had been rescued, took on an ominous job, and, launching its motor lifeboat circled the blazing ship in search of dead bodies. They found only four, and the crew had the grisly job of taking them on board, for the sole purpose of giving them a decent burial.

They were about to leave the scene when the **STELLAs** arrived. As Duff brought the **STELLA I** close to the **RIALTO** he could see the paint on his bridge begin to blister and stood off from the vessel by about 150 feet. The main salvage pumps were clutched-in to the main engines and great arc of water reached out over the midships accommodation. The **STELLA II** copied her example from the other side of the vessel. For the next twenty-four hours thousands of gallons of sea-water found their way on to the **RIALTO** from both tugs.

By this time the smoke had died down. A grappling hook was swung on board the forecastle, and one of the crew went up it. On his return, he reported to Duff, that as soon as he left the forecastle head, the decks were hot to the touch. Duff and Derek Brown decided to give the vessel another twelve hours soaking before they ventured on board. They changed the nozzles for a spray type and from then onwards, for the next eighteen hours both tugs motored slowly round the vessel spraying the decks and hull, by which time dawn had arrived. Duff and Derek Brown climbed up the rope ladder to survey the scene for themselves. The deck had cooled down sufficiently for them to walk on, but as the pair of them approached the midships the decks became increasingly warmer.

Donning the asbestos suits and breathing apparatus that they had brought with them, they ventured into the accommodation and up to the bridge. The bridge was a charred mass of wreckage ravaged by the fire. Even the compass was wrecked, where the oil in it had boiled and caused it to explode. All aluminium and brass fittings had melted. The once brightly polished telegraphs resembled a blobby-type mess on the floor of the bridge. All glass had melted out and lay in what looked like a black gooey mass. Retracing their steps to the accommodation, they found that all cabin doors, bunks and furniture had been ravaged by the fire and were reduced to ashes. Tracing their way to the engine-room, they found that there was thick palls of smoke still present and they found that there was still some smouldering remains that required quelling. They were unable to see the root of the fire or its extent due to the lack of visibility caused by the smoke.

The **STELLA II** tied up alongside, and, using her derricks, put her hoses on board. Hundreds of feet of hoses were coupled together so that the engine-room could be reached, and for a further four hours Derek Brown's team sprayed the engine-room with several hundred tons of water.

The following day they stepped on board to find that the previous days measures had not been in vain, and both the accommodation and engine-room were now free from smouldering remains, but by this time the **RIALTO** had taken on a list of some 10 degrees.

A ship-breaker at Marseilles had agreed to buy the wreck subject to the **RIALTO** being declared a total constructive loss. She was however, going to be difficult to tow, due to her list and the fact that she was riding low in the water, due to the thousand or so tons of water that had been pumped into her. The 8inch suction hoses that both tugs had on board were not long enough to reach the engine-room. So they were taken from the **STELLA II** and joined on to the end of those of the **STELLA I.** In this way, at least the **STELLA I** could start pumping while the **STELLA II** started the long tow. All went well, but they had to continue pumping her on to an even keel, outside territorial waters for fear of polluting the coastline. She was turned over the ship-breakers, declared a total loss, and finally towed in.

THE HORNCHURCH

The **HORNCHURCH**, a 4500ton tanker, in ballast, had been ploughing through heavy seas when her main engine suddenly started racing. Her 2nd Engineer instantly shut off the steam supply and the turbines came to a standstill. He guessed rightly when he told the Chief Engineer who had rushed down to the engine-room, that he reckoned that the ship had lost the propeller. As the vessel pitched and rolled, anyone who looked over the stern could clearly see that the important propelling unit had disappeared. As SOS was immediately sent out and within the hour the **HAINULT** was within hailing distance. The Captain of the **HORNCHURCH** felt that the ship was in no immediate danger, but allowed those of his crew who wished, to board the **HAINULT** when she came alongside.

The remaining crew took a light line along the bow and bit by bit a heavy towing cable was made fast to the capstan. The Captain of the **HORNCHURCH** agreed with Duff on a "daily hire" charge to tow the vessel to the nearest port of Oporto (W. Portugal) for dry-docking. Flashy radioed Oporto, only to find that the two dry-docks there were unavailable and would continue to be so for a further five weeks. He enquired about the dry-docks at the next nearest port, Lisbon, only to be told a similar story. This put the Captain in a bit of a quandary. The long tow to Falmouth in the UK or to Gibraltar were his only options.

He had not of course realised the ingenuity of the **HAINULT** personnel. On board the **HORNCHURCH** was a spare tailshaft complete with nut, key and, up high on the poop deck was a spare propeller, albeit a cast iron one complete with boss cone. In other words they had the gear but not the dry-dock, but they had Taffy. Flashy was instructed to radio Oporto to ask permission to enter the shelter of the dock area, and tie up to effect repairs. This permission was granted.

For the next eighteen hours they steamed slowly till they

met the calmer waters of Oporto where they entered and tied up to the quay. Very slowly the forward tanks were flooded to tip the vessel. This flooding had to be done slowly as the after tanks were partly drained, and the fuel oil bunkers transferred. The **HORNCHURCH** now lay with her foredeck almost awash, but her stern-tube lay just clear of the water.

Now Taffy and his 2nd Engineer and the **HORNCHURCH's** engineers could begin their work in the shaft tunnel, removing first the two sets of coupling bolts that connected the intermediate shaft to the engine and tail-shaft. These great big bolts, some three and half inches in diameter had to be removed using a slide hammer, and by the end of the day, the intermediate shaft and its bearings were cleared. The following day the **HORNCHURCH**'s Chief and his engineers started withdrawing the tailshaft, while Taffy and his engineers started getting the propeller ready for fitting, by cleaning and scraping its bore, and supervising its lifting up from the deck and over the stern. The dock-side crane was used to lower it down to water level. Around the stern of the **HORNCHURCH** in common with most ships, were brackets, carefully positioned for the purpose of attaching chain blocks for lowering the propeller in to position. Taffy and his engineers attached their chain blocks to these brackets and very slowly took the weight of the propeller from the dock-side crane. This was arduous work, as they were standing in the work-boat on one side and life-boat on the other, both were tied up to the rudder. Every time they pulled on the chain blocks the boats rocked and they all felt very unstable. By the following day they had managed to get the propeller in approximate position and the **HORNCHURCH** engineers were also in a position to start pulling in the replacement tailshaft. This too was an arduous task. Not only did the tailshaft have to be lifted up and aligned but it had to be slid into position, the shift in weight caused the stern to sink slightly lower into the water, albeit only an inch or so. But this caused water to start running along the stern tube and into the shaft tunnel. Fearing the inevitable danger of flooding of the engine-room space, the 2nd Engineer quickly decided to flood the fore-peak tank. In adding the extra 100 tons of water to the bow section the stern lifted sufficiently to prevent any further ingress.

When a tail-shaft is changed in dry-dock, the vessel would normally be on an even keel and therefore the sliding in, of the tail-shaft would be simply a matter of a horizontal pull. The **HORNCHURCH** was tipped and therefore the sliding in of the tail-shaft was a much more difficult position as it was up an incline of something approaching 10 degrees. This was a strenuous task even with so many hands. Bit by bit, foot by foot, the tail-shaft was drawn into the stern tube. Gradually it started emerging to the outside and it was then, that Taffy found that the key and key-way did not line up perfectly. This meant that the propeller had to be turned slightly. Taffy and his men lowered one side of the propeller while the other side was being raised in an effort to turn it slightly, their efforts were rewarded when the tail-shaft started sliding home. Inch by inch, it was pulled through till its thread was exposed on the outer face of the propeller.

The chain blocks supporting the propeller were taken down and a smaller one was suspended from the rudder post. The propeller nut that was to secure it was lowered over the side and into the work-boat using an eyebolt. It was now time to return to the **HORNCHURCH**. The stern gland was repacked as a precautionary measure, with its greasy packing, and, once this was done the fore-peak tank was pumped dry. At least now the fore deck would not be awash. The intermediate shaft bearings were replaced, followed by the intermediate shaft and the couplings were lined up. The coupling between the engine and the intermediate shaft had the bolts replaced and driven home, but it was found that the coupling between the tail-shaft and intermediate presented some problems. It was found that the bolt-holes although lined up were of a slightly different size.

Taffy, man of ingenuity, again came to the rescue, took two of the bolts to the **HORNCHURCH**'s engineer's workshop, and using the skills he had acquired during his apprenticeship machined steps on the bolts using the lathe. These two bolts were driven home as a temporary measure. Now the tailshaft was connected to the engine, he had other work to do, and he and his engineers were quickly back in the work-boat. Within minutes they were hauling up the great big 10" nut on to its thread. The main engine was turned by means of the turning gear, and slowly the nut wound its way along the thread. After what seemed like hours turning, the nut was firmly up against the boss of the propeller. Now the hard work really began. Around the curved surface of the nut were several grooves and on the boss face were several holes. One of the grooves had to be lined up perfectly with one of the holes, and a pegged key had to be lifted to prevent the nut coming loose.

Because neither had lined up in the fitting process, it now required some brute force. An enormous C-spanner was lowered into the work-boat complete with a 28lb. flogging hammer. With the work-boat rocking away, Taffy and his 2nd, took turns in driving round the nut till alignment of the key-way and hole was complete. Screws to clamp the key were put in, and all that remained was the positioning of the boss cone. The dockside crane was able to lower it down quite close to them and they were able to attach their lifting tackle to it with ease. Before it was finally positioned the Lloyds surveyor inspected the key that locked the nut to the propeller. A whole day was spent positioning the boss and at last the nuts were able to be tightened up.

The local dockyard sent two men to the ship who set up their boring gear and re-bored the coupling bolt holes, and as each hole was bored the bolts were driven home. The temporary bolts were removed and the last two holes bored and replacement bolts were fitted. This work was carried out over a two day period. In the meantime, the forward tanks were being pumped and the after tanks ballasted, so that the vessel could return to an even keel.

The Lloyds surveyor granted a seaworthiness certificate and the **HORNCHURCH** was able to continue her voyage to the Arabian Gulf having only lost a week.

THE SANDY WATERS

The **SANDY WATERS**, a 17000 ton bulk carrier in ballast, was ploughing south-wards through the Bay of Biscay. She was one of the new breed of vessels who flew a flag of convenience. She was registered in Liberia, thus avoiding many of the crippling taxes of other countries and was crewed by what appeared to be a league of nations. She had been built on the Tyne in 1950 as the **BRISTOL** had changed hands several times. She was proceeding to Lagos, Nigeria, to deliver 25km of 4" galvanised pipes in twenty metre lengths, for an oil refinery. She was then to make her way to South America to load bauxite. The 25km of piping was in four stacks on her deck and were held down with chains that were welded to the deck.

Because it was known that the **SANDY WATERS** would be experiencing bad weather on the voyage to Lagos, turnbuckles were fitted to each of the chains so that any slack that developed could be taken up. Daily the Chief Officer checked the chains, and not infrequently called on the Bosun to give the turnbuckles at least one turn with the crowbar.

The **SANDY WATERS** six cylinder Doxford engine gave her a comfortable cruising speed of 16 knots, and her engines in keeping with the whole of the vessel were kept in a reasonable condition, though the owners tried to keep her expenses restrained.

As she rounded Ushant on her leg across the Bay of Biscay to Cape Finisterre she met the ferocity of a whole gale (force 10), and her Master San Gan Lu decided that it would be prudent to cut the engine speed to about 10 knots. Visibility was low and he kept a look-out permanently posted on the radar, this crewman constantly changing the magnification from close range to long range. The **SANDY WATERS** pitched and rolled, so that sometimes the crewmen wished they had never set sail from Middlesborough. Quite often the bows went completely under and great big green seas swept her 700' long deck. Because of these seas no-one ventured on deck, and the checking of the deck cargo, they decided, could wait till the weather abated. In the face of the storm, a good course was held and after two long gruelling days crossing the Bay of Biscay the long distance radar showed Cape Ortegal on the port bow. Now was the time to alter course slightly to begin the passage down the coast of Spain and Portugal. This change in course was welcome as it meant that weather instead of being slightly abeam was directly over the bows, and although the vessel pitched even more she rolled less. Ten hours later she changed course again and this time she was heading almost due south. This meant that the heavy sea was abeam again and great big waves were pounding her decks.

Her Chief Officer Stefan Madeer, a Maltese, had just come on watch at 04:00, when above the roar of the wind, those on the bridge heard a terrific crack. As the Chief Officer looked down from the bridge he could see that one of the neat stacks of pipes was beginning to splay like a frayed rope at one end of the stack. The chain that for many days had bound it into position was nowhere to be seen. Summoning the Captain and the Bosun to the bridge he explained what he thought they ought to do. The decision taken by the Mate and the Captain was to head out directly into the Atlantic and when they had sufficient sea room, to turn the vessel towards the shore to give it a bit of lee so the deck crew could attempt to put a cable over the stack of pipes and winch it tight to secure it for the rest of the voyage.

Slowly they turned the vessel into the teeth of the storm, and, gradually her motion subsided. For four hours they steamed due west, by which time, they decided that when they had completed a 180 degree turn they would have about three or four hours working time to secure the cargo before they were in any danger. Now they had to manoeuvre the **SANDY WATERS** through the turn that would bring the storm over her stern. San Gan Lu brought the vessel round slowly, ever mindful of the sea now running abeam.

When they were half-way through the turning manoeuvre the Chief Officer and the helmsman both gave a high pitched scream as they both looked towards the starboard side. There, less than 1000 yards away was one of the great waves that the Mate had only dreamt of in his nightmares. There it was, about seventy feet high with its crest hovering to engulf anything that came within its reach. San Gan Lu, though very concerned about the ship, had met several giant waves in his eighteen years at sea. He knew that if the giant wave was a loner, there was little danger. When there was a set of three there was always problems, and he was busy scanning the surface of the sea with his binoculars. He felt reassured when he found that he could not see a second or a third big waves.

Still the vessel continued to turn as the "big wave" came even closer. Then came the moment of impact, as it hit the **SANDY WATERS**. It broke high over the superstructure aft, so that for a minute or two, those on the bridge only saw a solid wall of green water raining down in front of them. As it cleared they were mesmerised with the sight on deck. The stack of pipes that had previously been coming loose had vanished taking with it the stanchions on the ship's side. They were gratified to find that the remaining three stacks were still intact.

Minutes later the bridge was plunged into darkness, save for the emergency lighting. The wave had smashed through the engine-room skylights depositing hundreds of tons of water in the engine-room. It was not this that had caused the power failure, but the violent shock to the vessel had tripped out the switch-gear of the diesel generators. Both the 3rd and the 4th Engineers lay prone on the plates near to the main engine controls where they had been thrown about by the shock of the impact. Thirty seconds elapsed before the Chief Engineer found his way down to the switchboard, high up in the engine-room. As he pushed back the first breaker, it automatically tripped out again. One by one he took out some of the smaller circuit breakers to reduce the load, and finally managed to put the first breaker back on the board.

By this time one of the generators was beginning to run hot as the pump circulating it had stopped. He was able to put in the breaker for No.2 generator. Now at least he could replace the circuit breaker and get some semblance of order.

Ever mindful of his engine-room, the breaker for the engine-room auxiliaries was put in first. By this time he was joined by the 2nd Engineer who went down to the lower levels and started up the pumps one by one, before attending to the needs of the two engineers lying lifeless on the deck. They were being battered as they rolled around, one of them with a large gash across his head and the other with one leg laying at a peculiar angle.

The Chief began to get irate, as all the circuits were now working with the exception of the steering gear. Try as he did, the steering gear breaker refused to stay in. He climbed up the steps to investigate further and found that on entering the steering gear compartment, it was flooded to a depth of three feet and that the great twin motors connected to the hydraulic pumps were under water. This unfortunately, was one area of the whip where it was not possible to pump dry. There was a door that led directly to the engine-room, but it was held tightly shut by the weight of water. The upper doorway to the steering gear had been left open, and when the wave had broken over the vessel, the door had been wrenched off and the steering flat flooded.

The vessel, by this time had completed her turn and was now steaming, albeit slowly towards the Portuguese coast. The injured engineers were brought up as gently as possible to their cabins where their injuries were attended to, and the Chief engineer took some of the deck crew to the steering flat where he rigged up chain blocks, one end was attached to the steel watertight door and the other to a stanchion. After a lot of grunting and groaning the watertight door was pulled open a few inches and very quickly a lump of timber was placed in the opening. The water cascaded through the opening and down to the lower levels of the engine-room and found its way to the bilges. As the water level subsided, the men were able to open the door still farther and the flooding dropped to the level of the coaming. The junction boxes on each motor were opened up and dried using cotton waste and rags. These electric motors fortunately, were of the totally enclosed type, and when the Chief engineer arrived at the distribution board he experienced no difficulty in replacing the steering gear breaker. Now to San Gan Lu the vessel was again under complete command. One of the stringencies that the owners placed on the vessel was in the level of manning. She carried the Master and three deck officers, Chief engineer and three engineers, one Radio Officer, boatswain, carpenter and only nineteen crew, rather a small complement for a vessel of her size.

While the Chief Engineer and six of the crew had been busy, the remainder of the crew had been rigging up lifelines in an attempt to check the remaining stacks of pipes on the storm-swept deck. The "wave" had carried away the radio aerial, and the Radio Officer was attempting to rig another. One of the crew had perilously climbed the mast with a line, and was precariously perched in the crows nest, hastily hauling up a new one while the Radio Officer was running the free end to his transmitter. As soon as the connections were made he sent out a distress call saying that the vessel was in difficulties. Two men had been detailed to find baulks of timber to put over the engine-room skylights, as a considerable amount of rain-water was finding its way into the engine-room.

What no-one had noticed was that when the stack of pipes had gone overboard, they had taken away the overflow pipes to the fuel tanks, as well as the short stubby pipes and valves that were used to bunker the vessel. Nor had anyone noticed that as these were missing, that quantities of water were finding their way into the fuel tanks.

They were still approaching the Portuguese coast when generator No.2 started misfiring. The 2nd Engineer immediately went to the distribution board and removed the non-essential breakers to reduce the load, transferring it first to No.1 generator, before taking No.2 off the board. By this time the main engine started coughing a few times, only to pick up and resume its steady thump. The 2nd Engineer telephoned the bridge to inform them of the problems and the Radio Officer sent out a further distress signal. Within minutes the main engine was coughing badly, before it finally came to an abrupt stop, followed minutes later by No.1 generator. The Radio Officer sent out a further mayday signal which was intercepted by **STELLA I**. It read:-

FROM MASTER SANDY WATERS STOP AM WITHOUT POWER IN POS 41 78N 7.67E STOP DRIFTING EAST BY TWO KNOTS TOWARDS COASTLINE STOP REQUIRE TUG ASSISTANCE URGENTLY STOP ACKNOWLEDGE FROM MASTER STELLA I STOP AM SIX HOURS AWAY FROM YOU AND HAVE ALL THE POWER TO PULL YOU CLEAR

This was the weather for which the **STELLA**s had been built. They had been constructed so that men could move freely by passages from the midships accommodation to both bows and stern without being exposed to the weather. The foredecks were completely covered with strong steel casings so that they could work in the holds, completely covered and safe from the ravages of the elements. It was under these covers that the men were breaking out the heavy towing cables.

It was some time later that the Mate on the **SANDY WATERS** found the gaping 6" holes where the overflow pipes and the bunkering points had been, and informed the Chief Engineer. Due to the stringency of the labour force the vessel carried no ships carpenter, and one of the crew plugged the holes with lumps of wooden planking wrapped with sacking to prevent any further ingress of water. By now those on the bridge could see the coastline coming into view in the distance, and it was a formidable sight, as it was a rock-strewn coastline and the vessel was being blown towards its rocky shore. A further SOS was sent out which again was picked up by the **STELLA I**, and also by a French tug the **MOREAUX** who once before had had a brush with the **HAINULT**.

She was maintaining radio silence hoping to reach the **SANDY WATERS** before the **STELLA I**. She too was a powerful tug and could exert a 50 ton bollard pull against a 60 ton one from the **STELLA I** and her speed was the same as the two **STELLA**s. The Chief Engineer realised that the fuel oils, both heavy and diesel, were contaminated by sea water. With both the generators out of action he had no power to run the purifiers to de-contaminate the diesel oil.

It was normal practice, and the ship had been engined thus, to use diesel oil in the main engines for manoeuvring purposes. The exhaust gases were used to heat up the heavy oil, thus making it more fluid for pumping purposes. Once the heavy oil became liquid, a change-over valve was put into operation, and the main engine changed over to run on the cheaper oil, while the generators continued to run on the diesel oil.

The situation facing the engineers was to free the main settling tanks, high up in the engine-room, of the sea-water. The Chief and 2nd Engineer climbed up the ladders with wrenches in hand, undid the flange at the bottom of the diesel tank and allowed gallons of the fluid to run out and down to the engine-room deck, thus removing the water from the tank. Making good the flange connection and closing the valve, they descended to No.1 generator and released the connections to each of the fuel valves, and allowed the fluid to drain from each line. This action alone took twenty minutes, by which time the steep cliffs of the shore were less than a mile away, and some of the crew were panicking and standing by the lifeboats. The Chief Engineer went up to the settling tanks and opened the valve and allowed the precious fluid to run down the supply pipe and gush out of the fuel valve connections. One by one, the 2nd Engineer connected up each of the unions, and, slipping and sliding on the deck operated the hand pump that ensured the lubricating oil circulated the generator. At a pre-determined point, the Chief Engineer pushed the lever from air start to fuel oil and the generator burst into life.

A split second later the bow of the **SANDY WATERS** hit the first of the rocks, and now the bow was in contact with the rocks her stern began to drift round till she was abeam to the wind. As soon as the first impact was felt, San Gan Yu gave the order to abandon ship, and the Radio Officer sent off a message saying that the vessel was being abandoned. Before the vessel had swung round the starboard lifeboat was lowered and twenty or so of the crew clambered into it. This was easy to put into the water as it was on the lee side. The port side lifeboat was still feeling the full force of the storm and the first to be put into it were the injured men. It was then lowered towards the level of the water constantly being bumped against the ships side.

The vessel finally swung round and a rock pierced its side around the engine-room area, and the impact threw the Chief Engineer and 2nd to their feet on the platform above No.2 generator. As they saw the water level rising in the engine-room they too ran up the ladders and on to the deck. Skinning their hands in the process, they lowered themselves down the falls to the lifeboat below. This lifeboat fortunately had an engine in it and after a couple of swings it spluttered into life, and they quickly pulled away from the vessel. Half a mile away out to sea, they could see the other lifeboat with oars outstretched making heavy work against the waves. The motor lifeboat threw a line to the other and slowly they began to tow.

Hours later in the far distance they saw lights appearing through the gloomy night. First on the scene was the **MOREAUX** which passed within 50 yards of them, flashing by without stopping. Secondly was a Portuguese Rescue lifeboat from Oporto, which slowed down as soon as it sighted the lifeboats. Very cautiously they came alongside and the injured men were transferred, followed by the men from the 2nd lifeboat. While this was being done, the 3rd vessel the **STELLA I** lay alongside to provide a bit of shelter for the transfer operation. Only when the transfer was complete did Duff move off.

Duff knew that he was within an hours steaming from the **SANDY WATERS**, and seeing that the weather was at last beginning to lessen, and that the **MOREAUX** had a head start, decided that he would make a high speed run for the **SANDY WATERS**. Pushing the twin throttles forward, he unleashed power that churned the waters behind her. As she worked up to full speed, Duff lifted up the gates in front of the throttles and moved them halfway up into the red.

When he had been vying with the **MOREAUX** the first time, he had been on the **HAINULT** and had lost the battle of speed. Very slowly he began to catch up with the **MOREAUX,** and within ten minutes drew level. Rather than give the Frenchman a chance, he moved the throttles forward, moved the throttles to the top of the red. In doing the he knew he should not run for any length of time as it would eventually do some damage to the engines. As soon as he had the **SANDY WATERS** in view he brought the engines down to the top of the green and put the throttle gates back. He now had a good half a mile lead on the **MOREAUX** and as long as his crew managed to get a line on board, the prize was his. Luck was on their side, a grappling hook swirled round and up, to conveniently snag on an obstruction. Within minutes a couple of the crew were on board and a heavier line was made fast between the two.

In the distance they saw the **MOREAUX** burst through the gloom and slow down before turning round and once more disappearing. Duff felt that vengeance was sweet, remembering the **MOREAUX** had cheated them out of the salvage of the **CHOIX** by leaving survivors for the sake of greed.

The companion ladder was lowered on the port side and Duff and Ray George went on board. Ray George went straight to the engine-room where he found that it was flooded to a depth of about fifteen feet, as best he could guess. He also suspected some damage to the after part of No.6 hold adjacent to the engine-room, but was unable to tell as all the holds were in ballast. Duff found that No.1 hold was ruptured through striking the rocks and it was a safe bet that the fore peak tank had also suffered some damage. Duff decided that he would need considerable help and called up the **STELLA II** and the **HAINULT**. **STELLA II** said that she would be able to join her two days later when she had delivered her tow, and the **HAINULT** was on her way from Portsmouth and would be joining her in three days.

As the weather calmed the **STELLA** I tied up alongside and two great big mobile salvage pumps were hoisted on board to pump out Nos.2 and 5 holds. At the same time the tug put her own hoses into Nos.3 and 4 holds and used her own salvage pumps to keep the vessel on an even keel and prevent any sagging. A message was sent to the **STELLA II** to enquire where the nearest rock-free beach was to be found, and within hours they were informed by Derek Brown on the **STELLA II** that ten miles to the south lay just what they wanted. By this time the weather was completely calm and a day later found the level of the water in the holds dropping considerably. The following day found the **STELLA II** joining them and adding her pumping capacity to help discharge the ballast water.

Now the level of the water in the holds was low, it was time to try and move the **SANDY WATERS** Duff had the heavy towing cables taken on board and both **STELLA**s began to slowly haul the stern round till she lay at 90 degrees to the beach.

Now and only now, after all the time they had spent with the vessel could they inspect her properly from underwater. Duff donned the scuba gear and swam the short distance to the **SANDY WATERS**, where he finned his way downwards, and was amazed at what he saw. Along the starboard side just above the bilge keel for a length of about twenty feet, was a gash about 18" wide, and judging from its position extended from the engine-room to No.6 hold. This hole was too large to plate and was too extensive to cover or plug with wooden planking. Duff carried out an inspection of the ships length and found no more damage till he got near to the bows. There did not appear to be any damage to No.1 hold, but the bow stem right down to the keel was badly damaged. The bows appeared to be hard aground and apparently firmly wedged by rocks on either side.

Later that day the **HAINULT** sailed over the horizon to meet them. Taffy, forever a man of ideas, decided that the easiest way of re-floating the **SANDY WATERS** was to plug the hole. Taffy said that in the **HAINULT**'s hold was a huge roll of heavy gauge 000 canvas. It had been on board the vessel when she was the **4367** when both he and Duff and joined her. It had lain in the hold for all that time, and it was only when Taffy had boarded the **4368** that he was told that it was part of the standard gear for a deep-sea salvage tug. The Chief Engineer of the **4368** had explained how it was to be used. Now after all those years it was going to be put into practice.

For the next two days the Bosun and the carpenter were working together. What they produced, resembled a long sausage, some 25' in length and stitched or rather cobbled together. The inside of it was filled with a mixture of old hemp rope, unravelled and chopped into pieces, mixed with sacks of sawdust that had been deliberately split to allow the contents to disgorge.

The long sausage was draped along the deck of the **HAINULT**. Taffy went down into the engine-room of the **SANDY WATERS** with his scuba gear to inspect the hole in the vessel's side. The split had razor-like teeth along the whole of both edges. He noted all the obstructions that he would meet when he passed through the opening. Back on board the **HAINULT** they wiped him down with paraffin to remove all the oily mass which had adhered to him while he was on board the **SANDY WATERS**. Meanwhile steel cables were wrapped around the sausage-shaped plug at strategic points, and these in turn were attached to light lines. Early in the morning Duff and Taffy were over the side and finning their way down on one of their most dangerous missions. They trod water for a few minutes as they watched the movement of the water outside the gash in the ship's side.

As the water flowed into the vessel they could see nothing in particular, but as it was expelled, it came out with a certain amount of bubbles. Timing it for the moment the bubbles began to subside, they quickly dived for the gash in the side and found their way through the array of teeth. Taffy in the engine-room and Duff in No.6 hold. Both of them had to quickly find something to hang on to for dear life, to prevent themselves from being sucked back through those jagged edges. Duff quickly found himself a ladder at the after end of the hold and started climbing upward, taking the line with him, Taffy found himself hanging on to one of the runged platforms level with one of the generators. When he felt the suction subside, he started climbing up the ladder. Both of them had descended the depths with masks. For this fact alone Taffy was thankful, as the surface of the water in the engine-room had about 2" of oil floating on its surface which had obscured Taffy's vision by coating his mask.

Taffy's line was attached to two steel cables, and his and Duff's line were brought up on to deck. Slowly the lines were winched till the strain was taken by the steel cables. The long sausage was lifted up and over the side of the **HAINULT** and lay by the side of the hull. The winches continued hauling and gradually the sausage disappeared below the surface. Duff and Taffy were over the side again to make sure that the plug had been completely pulled into the hole for its whole length. It had.

Now the serious work of pumping out the engine-room and No.6 hold could begin. The two **STELLAs** with their powerful salvage pumps running took a day to pump them both dry. Taffy and Ray George went down into the engine-room to see the result of their handiwork, and were well pleased. The plug had been drawn by the action of the sea, at first, into the hole, then the cable had pulled it directly into the hole, and lastly, the sea had completed the work, by expanding the unravelled hemp rope and sawdust and shavings, till the whole plug expanded to the contour of the hole. They could both see by the rate that the water level was dropping at, that there was little if any ingress from the outside.

None of the tugs could venture near to the bows of the vessel for fear of the rocks, and their hoses, as long as they were, could not reach No.1 hold. The only method of pumping was to use the mobile salvage pumps. The decision was made to attempt to tow the **SANDY WATERS** off the rocks. The following day they put their heavy towing cables back on board the stern of the vessel and both of them drew off some 500 yards distant. One by one their anchors were taken by the **HAINULT** and taken a further 100 yards out and dropped. This operation alone was a long days work. The following morning the two **STELLAs** started moving out till their cables were bar tight, both of them heaved for about a half hour and no recovery was made. In frustration Duff order top of the red for both tugs and for the next fifteen minutes the froth boiled away from their sterns, still without success, and they shut the engines down. Both Duff and Derek Brown thought at one time that they were actually making progress. A 40 ton pull was registered by both tugs, and this gave a speed of one and half knots over the bottom, this dropped and dropped and then went into the red signifying that the cables were stretching, and then recovering and drawing the sterns backwards.

THE CONTINUATION OF THE SANDY WATERS

That afternoon with a bag of explosives, Taffy set out with several others in the work-boat, and anchored within 30ft of the rocks where the bows were firmly embedded. Taffy was over the side, and for once became a bit frightened, as he was swept by the current between the rocks. Jamming himself between two rocks, he arranged three packs of explosive around the base of the large rock on one side of the bow. Forcing a 20 minutes time-delay fuse into the middle of each of the packs, and noting the time on his watch, he waited for the undertow to haul him out of his cubby-hole and swam back to the work-boat. The short trip back to the **HAINULT** took a further ten minutes. He shouted to the two **STELLA**s to start hauling as the detonations were imminent, and their sterns started boiling away immediately.

When the explosion came, the bows of the **SANDY WATERS** disappeared from view, as an enormous fountain of water erupted. They hauled away for the next ten minutes without success. An hour or so later found the work-boat making its way to the same spot, with the crew pulling out any decent sized fish that they came across. They were under strict orders from Angel not to let anything go to waste, and they even pulled out a few eels that he announced that he would turn into jellied eels.

On reaching the site, Taffy was amazed to find that the three charges had removed a large amount of the rock, and decided to place another three charges around the now-gaping hollow in the rock, again giving them a 20 minutes delay fuse. Climbing back on board the **HAINULT**, they witnessed the same sort of eruption of water at the bows, but with the **STELLA**s hauling away there was a terrific groaning, as the **SANDY WATERS** slid off the rocks. As the vessel slid off and into deeper water her bow came down till her deck, aft of the forecastle head rode only about two feet above the sea. The **HAINULT** quickly went alongside and lowered her hoses into the hold and started pumping. Hours later, they noted that the water level in No.1 hold had neither decreased nor increased, indicating that her pumps were only matching the ingress of water. The **HAINULT** cast off, and with a lot of difficulty to those on board both vessels, the **STELLA I's** towing cable was transferred to the **HAINULT** and the **STELLA II** started using her salvage pumps. With the **HAINULT** doing the towing, the **STELLA I** brought in her towing cable and joined the **STELLA II** at the bows and she too started pumping No.1 hold. An hour later it was noted that the bows were riding higher indicating that they were taking out more water than was entering the vessel.

Two hours later found them nearing the beach where they were going to bring the **SANDY WATERS** ashore, but it was not yet high tide. The **STELLAs** continued pumping while the **HAINULT** turned the vessel. At high tide the **STELLAs** pushed their charge into the shallows of the beach till there was only feet beneath their bottoms. At this point they removed their hoses and went off into deeper water to anchor leaving the **HAINULT** to push the vessel the last fifty or so yards, grounding her.

At low tide she drained out all but a few feet of water and they flocked on board. Angel, as usual raided the pantry and the stores so that he was able to change their diet for a week or so. The fore-peak tank was indeed badly ruptured and so too was the collision bulkhead, which accounted for the flooding of No.1 hold.

Damage to the fore-peak tank was so extensive that it was beyond them to affect repairs, but the collision bulkhead could be repaired. The access to the fore-peak tank was via a hatch that was about two feet square. The 10mm sheet that all three tugs carried were all 8' x 4', and it was decided to cut two of these sheets into 4' x 2' before taking them on board. This operation was costly as it prevented them from working at low tide, but at least they were able to get them on board the vessel in time for the next tide.

While Taffy and the engineers were busy, the deck crew were busy unshackling the anchor chain from the anchor. The chocks securely held the anchors, but the chain was pulled up slightly so that parts of them now lay on the deck. Ray George in the meantime had a mobile generator hoisted on to the deck, which he had connected to the switchboard and now had running. The windlass was used to drag up the anchor chain from the chain locker till both lay in piles on the deck. One of the after winches was put into operation, and, one by one, using a cables, the anchor chains were winched along the deck till they fell into No.5 hold. This action reduced the weight in the bows and would be an aid to buoyancy. However Ray George's ardent wish was to get at least one of the generators running, but he dismissed this idea when he saw the condition of the motors themselves. The commutators of each motor were covered in a velvet of oily grease when the flooded engine-room had been pumped down.

Then he had an idea. He had seen car engines cleaned by the use of steam jets. Alongside was the **HAINULT**, and there lay an adequate supply of steam. A small rubberised canvas hose was attached to a suitable steam supply and on the end of the hose was, attached a 1/2" gate valve with a 2ft length of tube with the inner end screwed into the valve. The other end he flattened out to give it a fan shape. As he opened the valve, water gushed forth and as it cleared itself, he was met with a fan-shaped blast of steam. He directed it at the armature first slicing the steam jet through the field windings and lastly on to the commutator. Within a few minutes the areas that he had cleaned, glistened, and he turned his attention to No.2 generator and repeated the process.

By the time he had completed No.2, he was itching to try out No.1 generator, and finding sufficient starting air, called one of the crew to operate the lubricating oil pump primer. Pushing the starting lever from air start to fuel, the generator coughed twice before settling in to a steady rhythm. He decided that it was prudent to let it run for an hour or so as the revolving action alone would act like a spin-drier and evacuate any water left in the motor. He went in search of the circulating water pumps for the generator, these too he found to be badly contaminated in the same way, and were treated to the gift of the steam hose. He knew that this motor would need at least 24 hours to dry out and went in search of the compressor. This was situated high up in the engine-room and had escaped the ravages of the flooding. With the mobile generator still connected, the compressor was used to pump up both reservoirs of starting air.

By this time the three lower plates in the fore-peak tank had been welded into position and no more work could be done there as the advancing tide was flooding the tank. As the tide rose still further those on board the tugs were surprised to find that the **SANDY WATERS** began to float freely. There was a problem, though, with this happening, the water level in the fore-peak tank was only one foot below the level of the last plate that had been welded into position. The **SANDY WATERS** was brought out into deeper waters and the **STELLA II** hoisted her derrick and swung it outboard so that it could take the weight of the port anchor. When she had the weight, the remainder of the anchor chain was un-chocked and lowered to water level. Then the **STELLA II** moved slightly away and aft and deposited the anchor in No.5 hold. This action was repeated on the starboard anchor. By the time the anchors had been removed the "freeboard" in the forepeak tank had increased to two feet.

It was agreed by all, that having got this far with the venture, it would be better to beach the vessel once more to finish the welding of the plates. A couple of hours later found them beaching **the SANDY WATERS** for what they hoped was the last time. This time they beached her beam-on to the beach, and as the tide fell she was left high and dry. Two more plates were welded into position and these reached up to the top of the fore-peak tank. As the tide came up the **SANDY WATERS** gently floated off and with the main towing cable made fast to the windlass, the **STELLAs** began to haul away from the land.

The **HAINULT** was tied up alongside aft to keep up the supply of steam for cleaning purposes. Between them Taffy and Ray George steam cleaned every motor that had been subjected to the flooding, and many of the plates had been cleaned in the same way. At least now they could walk more easily. Previously all movement around the engine-room was hazardous, moving up and down ladders was treacherous. Ray George had shut down No.1 generator down the previous day when he had found that he could not use the circulating pump,. He now started the pump, only to find the motor hummed steadily, though it did spark a bit. Then he and Taffy started up No.1 generator. He shut down the mobile generator and disconnected it's leads, and coupled up the leads of Nos.1 and 2 generators to the distribution board. After a few minutes he gingerly attempted to put it on the distribution board. He and Taffy were both expecting the breaker to jump out as soon as it was engaged, and were pleasantly surprised when it stayed on the board. One by one they engaged the switches that would allow the auxiliary circuits they engaged the switches that would allow the auxiliary circuits to operate. Again the circulating pump was started up and the flashing of the commutator had ceased. The steering gear was put into operation.

Ray George and Taffy agreed that before anything else was done they should start purifying the diesel oil supplies. They felt reasonable with the tank that they were using, but it would not last forever. the first thing to be done was to pump up the dirty diesel tank from the ship's double bottom tank, then run it down through the purifier and up to the ready use tank, high up in the engine-room. While this was being done, the compressor was working away for hours on end pumping up the main engine starting air reservoir. Their intention was for the vessel to proceed under her own power.

The intention of all was to bring the **SANDY WATERS** to the UK and leave it to the court of arbitration to sort out. Being registered in Liberia for convenience, any arbitration court there would have taken a year to come to any decision, and would invariably find in favour of the owner rather than the salver.

When the second ready-use tank was full, the generator fuel supply was changed over to this tank, and the first tanks contents were allowed to empty by gravity into the ship's double-bottom tank. This took the best part of five hours, by which time the main engine starting air reservoir was fully charged. No.2 generator was started and within minutes was put on the board, and the main engine turning gear was engaged.

The fuel oil valve lines were loosened at each joint adjacent to the valve and a five gallon oil drum was placed under each line. For hours the engine was turned and the contents of each line were drained. While the main engine was being turned the main engine lubricating oil pumps were operating to ensure an even distribution of oil around the engine. The main engine was now drawing it's supply from the same tank as the two generators. When Ray George checked the contents of the five gallon drums he found that it was heavy fuel oil which certainly contained a fair amount of oily water. Emptying all the drums one by one into the oily bilge, the drums were replaced in their original positions. A further hours elapsed before he checked them again. This time the contents were badly stained diesel oil that still contained a small amount of water. This too was dumped in the oily bilge, and for yet another hour the engine turned slowly. After an impatient hours wait, he checked yet again the contents of each drum and was pleased to find that although the diesel oil was still stained slightly there was no water present.

There was still more preparatory work to be done. The main engines, being oil engines had their lower half totally enclosed and therefore most likely un-contaminated, but Ray George was a bit concerned about the possibility of the lubricating oil being contaminated. The lubricating oil passed through a bank of filters of varying types. The oil supply to each was shut off and he opened up each filter looking first for any water and secondly for the telltale yellowish emulsion that always proved that it was possible to mix oil and water. He was relieved to find none.

Turning gear out, the control level was pushed to air start and the minute the engine turned progressed to fuel on. The great big engine coughed and fired a few times before coming to a halt. The compressors were put into operation to pump up the main engine reservoirs again, and they had a further wait of four hours before they could make a fresh attempt, and the turning gear was once more engaged to keep the engine turning and the oil circulating. On the next attempt, each cylinder coughed and fired and the engine settled down to its gentle thump, as the great big pistons went up and down. Now the starting air was automatically being charged up. Gradually Ray George increased revolutions.

Bill Samuels on the bridge, apart from seeing the smoke billowing from the funnel, felt the vessel become alive. Those on the tugs, who spotted the smoke billowing from the **SANDY WATERS** let out a cheer. Minutes later the smoke diminished to a thin whisper. As Ray George increased revolutions till further, those on the bridges of the **STELLAs** felt their vessels leap forward as the towing load came off. They fanned out and the crewmen on the **SANDY WATERS** cast off the heavy towing cables, so that they could be drawn on board and stowed.

All this time the **HAINULT** had been sailing alongside the vessel, while she was being towed. Now it was better to cast off and act as escort.

When a check was made on the amount of fuel they had, it was found that if the heavy fuel was used, they had plenty, but there was insufficient to make the trip to the UK just using diesel oil. It was suspected that the heavy fuel oil was contaminated and therefore should not be used. Arrangements were made to call in at Coruna to dump the remainder of the oil at the depot there and re-bunker for the remainder of the trip. On this call to Coruna, arrangements were also made for the replacement of the overflow pipes and bunkering valve stems. The breakage of which was the vessels original cause of her problems.

Repairs and bunkering took two days, during which time the mobile generator was lowered on to the **HAINULT**'s deck and she transferred it to the **STELLA II**, and all other gear was removed. Soundings were carried out in all holds and found that the bulkhead repairs were holding up well. A Lloyds surveyor granted a temporary sea-worthiness certificate for the vessel, and the **SANDY WATERS** set sail for her last leg to Falmouth.

The waste heat boiler up in he funnel was doing it's work and some hours later the steam coils had heated up the heavy oil sufficiently for the oil to be pumped up to the main settling tanks where the exhaust gases would heat it to a high enough temperature to allow it to be used on the main engine. Four hours later Ray George affected the change-over from diesel oil to heavy fuel oil without any problems.

Now that everything in the engine-room was running as it should be, the boiler was put to other uses, and the remainder of the main engine and generators were steamed to remove the oil streaks and the remainder of the deck plating and pumps. By the time the operation was complete everything looked in pristine condition. The bilges and the oily-bilges had by this time collected an enormous amount of debris and oily water, and Ray George made sure that the contents of all bilges were pumped up to the oily-water separator. This was a lengthy process as the suctions were frequently blocked.

Days later the **SANDY WATERS** entered Falmouth and took up residence in the River Fal. The owners, had of course been contacted through agents, as soon as the vessel had been pulled off the rocks, and they were complaining bitterly, through the agents, that the pipes had not been delivered to Lagos. Apparently the owners were being sued by the Lagos Authorities for non-delivery and were anxious to claim the cargo of pipes, more so that they were the ship itself. Duff's understanding was the same as the B.o.T, that the cargo and the vessel were all part of a salvage package.

The owners were pressing for an early sitting, which suited the H.T.C. admirably, and a date for a month hence was set for the hearing. Duff, Taffy and Ray George were in court on the appointed day. A careful log of what had happened on board the vessel had been kept by Ray George, from the time that they had arrived on the scene, and this was read out in court. San Gan Lu was telling his side of the story, and was exonerated from all blame. A Lloyds surveyor gave an explanation of his written report of his findings. The lawyer representing the owners tried his hardest to de-rate what had taken place at the scene, pointing out that the vessel could have been towed home rather than under her own power, etc. In the end the judge ruled that due to the actions of the H.T.C. and the Portuguese Lifeboat Service, there had been no loss of life. The vessel **SANDY WATERS** had not only been saved by the prompt action of the H.T.C. but it had been brought to port. Based on his findings he had decided to award 40% of the hull value. At this the lawyer representing the owners leapt to his feet, saying that he was lodging an appeal. This appeal was lodged the same day, but withdrawn the next day. It was then that they learnt from the papers that the owners were those of the **CERCUR**, the Papadolus Brothers.

THE FREDRICCSEN

The **FREDRICCSEN** had docked at Harwich and had discharged her passengers in the afternoon. The crew had cleared up and a shore gang had been on board doing the cleaning of the cabins. Stores had been brought on board and had carefully been stowed. The following morning the Danish vessel was to take on 500 tourist class passengers and 150 1st class passengers for a ten-day cruise round the Baltic Sea. She was scheduled to do this throughout the summer season.

Many of the crew were ashore as it would be a further ten days before they were able to do it again. As one of the crew was passing through the 1st class accommodation he noticed a thin wisp of smoke coming from one of the alleyway ventilators. The **FREDRICCSEN** was a pre-war built vessel and the fire warning devices were few and far between. The few engineers that were on board, started all the powerful pumps in the engine-room and connected them to the deck lines. The fire alarm was sounded and the water jets were directed into the ventilator ducting. In the meantime the shoreside Fire Brigade was summoned, and some 45 minutes later two fire appliances arrived. By this time most of the 1st Class accommodation was fiercely ablaze. For the next twelve hours the appliances continued to pour thousands of gallons of sea water at the blazing vessel.

A signal was sent out for a fire-fighting tug to attend the scene. The nearest one at that moment was stationed at Dover, so the **STELLA I** offered her services, as she too had had powerful fire-fighting jets. She was in the Thames at the time. She set off and was soon chasing round towards Harwich at half-way into the red. She arrived two hours after the fire brigade and she too started pouring water on to the vessel from the seaward side. By morning those in attendance could see that the continual dousing was having a definite effect on the vessel as the fire was beginning to peter out. They also noticed that the colossal volume of water that had been poured on to her also had another effect, she had taken on a decided list. There were no flames on the ship but thick palls of smoke were still emanating from the Ist Class accommodation and it was imperative that this was fully doused. By noon there was an absence of smoke, but the **FREDRICCSEN** now lay on her beam ends and at low tide her port propeller was clearly visible. The two fire appliances stayed in attendance for the rest of the day and evening in case the fire broke out again. It did not.

Two days later the **STELLA II** and the **HAINULT** arrived on the scene to begin salvage operations. A price of one million Danish Kroner was agreed for the righting of the vessel, and daily hire from then onwards. The arrival of the other two tugs brought six camels to the site. For the next ten days divers were down on the sunken vessel pulling through heavy cables through parts of the accommodation both midships and aft. When these had been threaded through them, they were attached to heavy duty chains. For the next two tides the divers were down there easing the chains past the various obstacles till both ends were outside the ship. Two camels were shackled aft and two more midships. A further one was shackled to the anchor chain.

At high tide the camels were evacuated of water by the compressors and very slowly the masts of the **FREDRICCSEN** started rising out of the water till the vessel lay there with a list of some sixty degrees. By this time the camels were level with the surface of the water, but the vessel was still not afloat. As the tide receded, down went the divers to shorten up the chains attached to the camels. This shortening-up took a further two days. The following day fortunately coincided with a spring tide and when the camels were eventually evacuated, the masts moved through an arc till the vessel only had a twenty degree list, but still she did not float. At low tide her decks were still awash, and it was decided to wait for a week for the next neap tide when it was hoped that her decks would be clear of water. A rest was taken by all for few days and when the neap tide arrived her decks just cleared the water and immediately the **STELLA**s and the **HAINULT** put their hoses on board. The **STELLA** s' were placed in the vast cavity of the engine-room while the **HAINULT** placed hers in the baggage hold. As **the** oily water spewed out of the tugs' sides the tide began to rise and with it up came the **FREDRICCSEN**.

By the time the tide was full, the vessel had about three feet of freeboard to both decks. A further eight hours pumping of the engine-room resulted in only a 12inch gain in freeboard. By this time she still had a twenty degree list. When Taffy and Duff went onboard the vessel they found that the engine-room contained a mountain of mud on one side. They also found that most of the accommodation on the same side was impassable, also being filled with mud. It was the same story with the baggage hold, and was indeed going to be a problem to clear. The **HAINULT** tied up alongside and with her pumps running, hosed out the cabins in the upper deck. Stairways had to be blanked off with plates to prevent the water and mud travelling down to the lower decks. Meanwhile the **STELLA I** put her hoses down to the engine-room and the water jets were directed at the mountain of mud to loosen it. Gradually over the course of a week, great globs of mud found their way to the lower levels of the engine-room where it was hastily sucked up by **STELLA II**'s hoses. This work took a whole week, by which time the vessel's list decreased to only fifteen degrees. The next to be given the same treatment was the baggage hold. This section took a further three days to clear and did not significantly affect the list.

The colossal volume of mud locked into the lower levels of the accommodation was certainly going to be a mammoth operation to remove. The Danish Shipping Company required the vessel to be towed to Copenhagen, but the Lloyds Surveyor would not grant a certificate to tow the vessel till the vessel's list was reduced to at least five degrees.

The mud that was left in the upper accommodation was

now beginning to dry out, thus forming a cakey-clay mixture. This was easier to remove, but was certainly labour intensive. Taffy, man of resource, went along to the Job Centre and hired twenty labourers to dig the stuff out and place in wheelbarrows, which were then tipped over the side into a barge alongside. The stairways that had previously been blanked off with plates were now opened up and the labourers were able to descend to the second deck level. The mud in this level had not caked but was of a slimy consistency. Taffy brought in one of the **HAINULT**'s 4inch hoses and lowered the hose into the slimy mud. The **HAINULT** was equipped with reciprocating steam pumps and although they worked apparently slowly, they could still pump large volumes. For the first day they had to continuously move the hose about from cabin to alleyway and in to the next cabin. On returning to the vessel the following morning, Taffy found that the area that they had cleared the previous day was now covered in the slimy mud again, as it had drained from the rest of the accommodation and was to a depth of about three feet on the whole of the deck, and in doing so the list had reduced still further. What they needed was some more pumps of the same type. The local waterworks were contacted and they came to the rescue. They supplied them with two diesel driven slow acting diaphragm pumps. These pumps had previously been used for the draining of holes that had been dug in roads. With both of these running and the **HAINULT**'s, they were able to clear all off the mud from the second deck. By this time, the list had reduced to just under ten degrees.

It was imperative the mud was removed from the lowest deck. The same pumping arrangements were used to clear this deck. As the days progressed, the list gradually decreased till the majority of the mud was removed, and the list of the vessel decreased to only three degrees. The Lloyds Surveyor granted a certificate of seaworthiness and the **FREDRICCSEN** was ready to leave for her tow across the North Sea. A portable generator was put on board and coupled up to the steering gear and the lights on the main deck and the two **STELLAs** started the tow back to Copenhagen.

THE END OF HAINULT TOWING COMPANY

Ever since the clearance of the sunken vessels in the Elbe, Duff, Taffy, Bill Samuel's and Derek Brown were made aware by the various agents, that there was a nameless consortium who were showing a consistent interest in the company. All that was ever said was, "Have you ever thought about selling out to the Arabs"? As far as they knew the only Arab towing concerns were operating out of Alexandria, both salvage and ocean towage. One evening when the two **STELLAs** were towing an enormous barge loaded with pipes and girders for the construction of a pier in the Isle of Wight, and the **HAINULT** was about ten miles behind with a smaller barge that was filled with drilling equipment for the same site, Duff received a radio message inquiring as to whether they were interested in a two-year contract in the Mediterranean. Duff radioed back to say that they were interested and requested more details.

The following day they received a long telex laying out the conditions. Taffy was a bit dubious as to whether they would ever be paid, as he had heard many bad tales about the Arab nation as a whole. A few days later they were again towing barges to the same site with equipment and cement when they received a message from their agent in the Isle of Wight saying that he had received a draft contract from the consortium.

The contract was to clear the whole of the Libyan coastline of all damaged vessels. Most of the wrecks had been left over from bombings during the war. Having cleared the River Elbe of all obstructions they felt that this contract would be a repeat process.

On arrival in Ryde with their tows, they went directly to the agents office to read the draft contract. They had two more trips to make with barges and pontoons before they were free of all contractual responsibilities. Both Duff and Taffy signed and stated that they would arrive at Tripoli six weeks hence. They felt that all three vessels should dry-dock and overhaul a lot of their gear in preparation for two years continuous work. During dry-docking all crew members and officers (with the exception of Masters and Chief Engineers) went off for a fortnights leave.

Weeks later they set off, towing the camels behind them, for the long trip to Tripoli, bunkering as usual at Tangiers, where they saw that the **CHEYNEY** was still tied up to the breakwater. Days later they sailed into Tripoli harbour to meet their new agent for instructions. The instructions were simple:- Remove all obstructions, visible and under the surface along the whole of the Libyan coastline.

Tripoli was a shallow draught harbour and in common with all Mediterranean ports had a rise and fall of tide of no more than 4inch. There were three vessels of between 1500 and 2000 tons that were sitting on the bottom in about twelve feet of water. The cargo in the undamaged holds had been cleared but there was several feet of water in each of these holds. This meant that the **HAINULT** would have to do the discharging of the damaged hold as there was insufficient draught for the **STELLAs** to operate. The scavengers had been on board each of the vessels and had removed all brass fittings and copper tube and in doing so, all winches and windlasses were inoperable. Amongst the gear brought out with the **STELLAs** were some powerful electric winches and the **HAINULT** transferred these on board the vessels. For days those on board laboured under the intense heat of the Libyan summer sun, to fit the winches in position and rig up the lifting cables. The **STELLA I** brought round two large barges that were warped alongside each vessel in turn, and for weeks the crew and locally recruited labour feverishly laboured to raise the sodden cargo and transfer it to the barges. This was slow work as frequently the divers had to go down into the hold to fix wires to the cargo. About a month later all three vessels were completely cleared and patching up could start. In most cases the explosions had taken place within the vessels (due to bombing) and the ragged edges were on the outside of the hulls. This meant that a load of 10mm plate had to be brought across from the **STELLAs** and lowered into the holds and placed in position whence it could be clamped. This work took a further two weeks at which time pumping could begin. As the **HAINULT's** pumps drained the first of them she floated easily and was towed a short distance seaward so that the **STELLA I** could complete the draining and could continue the tow. The second was pumped dry by the **HAINULT** and stubbornly refuse to float off. It was found that she had devoured a large quantity of sand through her holing. The workboats were used to ferry messenger ropes and finally the main towing cables from both **STELLAs**.

Both the tugs at an extreme distance moved very slowly and with their sterns frothing away dragged the vessel into deeper water.

One of the tugs directed her hoses into the holds to loosen up the sand while the other was pumping each hold in turn. Over the course of a couple of days the bulk of the sand was removed from each hold. The same treatment was given to the third vessel and met with success.

The nearest ship-breaker was at Algiers and they agreed to take all vessels that were salvaged there, although the prices quoted were rock bottom. The journey with the three vessels was a slow one as they had to stop numerous times to pump out water that was finding its way into each of the vessel. This short trip took them eight days to accomplish.

On returning to Tripoli harbour, a small coaster of some 300tons was raised using the camels, and two barges were raised, after their cargo had been removed using the grabs. There remained two coasters that were so badly damaged that they were beyond refloating. It was decided to blast them apart. This really was a last resort alternative, as the port had to be cleared of all craft large and small that were in the harbour. Gigantic fountains of water gushed up into the sky as the explosions took place. For the next few weeks great chunks of steel plates and sections of masts were raised by the **HAINULT** and placed in barges before being ferried round to Algiers. At last the port of Tripoli was clear of obstructions.

Further along the coast was a 2000ton ship that was on the beach high and dry, with a hole either side of the engine-room that was about five foot square.

The problem was that these holes could easily be plated up but the vessel could never reach the water. It was decided to break up the vessel in position. The vessel had two holds forward and one aft, with the engine-room amidships. Taffy, man of ideas, put forward a plan. His idea was to cut the ship up into three sections, cutting through the ships hull leaving the holds as two separate sections and possibly these could be towed off the beach and floated away.

There were no problems cutting through the sides and the upper deck nor even through the tank tops in the engine-room, but the lower parts of the tanks and the ship's bottom were going to be a real problem. The tanks were still full of water, and these were pumped dry by using long hoses attached to a mobile salvage pump. Access holes were cut to allow Taffy and his men to lay down while they were cutting their way through the ship's bottom. They were working in a very confined space, with very little ventilation, and as the oxy-acetylene flame cut through the plate there were small explosions as the flames came into contact with the wet sand underneath. These 'pops' occurred every inch or so and was very disconcerting. The first day of cutting found that they had only cut about a quarter of the way round from each side.

On returning to the **STELLA I** they found their agent on board with two Arabs dressed in the traditional thoub and with long flowing gutras. Taffy bowed, he didn't know what he was supposed to do. Their spoken English was impeccable. Hassan Kamel introduced himself and straight away set down to business. His partner, Yousef Abdullah said, "Mr Duff, Mr Jones, I represent a consortium that has both Arab and Greek interests. You, of course know of the Papadoulos brothers and we have many other partners along the coast of North Africa. We control much of the shipping that operates in the Mediterranean and we wish to buy you out. Your company's name is legend in these parts since you removed the **CERCUR** and raised the U-boat. Yes, Mr Duff we even knew about that. You have a reputation that is second to none. We wish to buy you out at the half-way point in your contract, and in the following year we wish to have some of out members working with you, so that they too, can learn the trade and eventually take over the tugs, and the running of them by the end of the contract. The Papadoulos Brothers have advised us that to offer you any less than five million pounds sterling, would be an insult. Please advise the agent when you wish to discuss the idea any further".

Work continued on cutting up the ship into three sections. A bulldozer was hired and brought to the site on a low loader. The bulldozer ploughed out a pool between the sea and the vessels side till there was about three feet of water. At the same time the mobile pumps were pumping out the remaining water from the foreholds. Meanwhile, over the course of two days, laborious work had taken place in hauling across the main towing wires that could be fastened to the windlass. A heavy bridle was spliced so that all three tugs could haul away at the same time. Two days later, early in the morning, all three tugs started hauling on the bow section. As soon as movement was detected they changed tack and started pulling out to sea. They were surprised at how easily she slid off the beach and into deeper water. Taffy, as soon as the vessel was afloat came alongside in the work-boat and clambered up the rope ladder to see if the holds were making any water. He was pleasantly surprised to find that they were bone dry. The vessel was devoid of anchors, so the **HAINULT** tied up alongside and remained at anchor.

The aft section contained a shaft tunnel and although there was a watertight door to the tunnel, Taffy had reservations as to how watertight it really was. He therefore welded it up to make sure. The shaft itself was cut through and the opening was plated over as well..

While this was being done, the towing cables had been attached to capstans on the shore side of the poop deck and the two **STELLA**s started hauling. The aft section did not want to move as easily as the fore section, and it was only when the throttles were pushed well into the red zone did the after-section begin to move. Inch by inch it slid into the water till it floated. Now all that remained was the centre section complete with what was left of the bridge and the engine-room.

The two Arabs found their way on to the **HAINULT** that evening and asked Duff if he and Taffy had considered the offer. Taffy and Duff had discussed it at length each evening and had decided that they would indeed sell out. They were both well into their forties and they felt that it was time to settle down to a life that was less gruelling. Hassan Kamel said, "Mr Duff, Mr Jones, You have not jumped at the offer, I therefore concede that the offer was not enough. I am therefore empowered to offer you six million pounds sterling and a terminal gratuity of 20% of the value of everything that you salvage during the remainder of your contract, but I need an answer now". Duff looked at Taffy and he nodded. "We accept", said Duff.

A crane with a caterpillar trick was brought to the site on a low-loader, and as the various parts of the bridge and hull were cut up, they were lifted up and placed on the low-loader. Each afternoon the low-loader set off for Tripoli where an enormous pile of scrap metal was beginning to accumulate. **STELLA I** set off for Algiers with the aft section in tow, while the **STELLA II** started towing the fore section to Tripoli where it was moored to the quay.

Meanwhile Taffy and his men found that they could produce more scrap metal that the low-loader could transport, so another one was hired. Removing the remains of the engine was not a difficult job as they simply flame-cut through nuts and bolt to save undoing them. By the time they had reached the tank tops the pile of scrap iron that had been transported to the quay at Tripoli, was rapidly diminishing as it was loaded into the fore holds. Cutting up the lower parts took a further week and Taffy had reckoned that they had used up eighty cylinders of oxygen and thirty of acetylene to complete the job. The last load departed for Tripoli and the low-loader returned to take back the crane. Bill Samuel's looked at the beach for the last time before he and Taffy set sail for Tripoli where the **HAINULT** and the **STELLA II** were to tow the fore section with its cargo to the breakers.

When they arrived at Tripoli, they were greeted by Yousef Abdullah, dressed not in his Arab attire but in naval whites, sporting three gold rings of First mate. With him were several other Arabs and a few others who were lighter skinned and later turned out to be Greeks. "We are joining your vessels, Mr. Samuels, so that we can find out all about the business". Late the following day, the last of the scrap iron had been loaded and they sailed in tandem, towing the loaded fore section for Algiers. After handing over the hulk they took the opportunity of re-bunkering.

Further along the coast towards Benghazi there was a small coaster of some 300tons that was sitting on the bottom with her decks nearly awash. Taffy and Duff were over the side immediately, to examine its hull, and after extensive searching found no holes in the hull at all. This being the case that it only required pumping the two **STELLAs** departed for Benghazi harbour leaving the **HAINULT** to carry out the salvage. It was not known how the vessel had managed to get into its present position, nor how so much water got into her.

The **HAINULT** tied up alongside and put her hoses into the two holds and began pumping. For two days the water level dropped as the holds were pumped and the cargo was exposed. It consisted of cylindrical metal objects about 9" in diameter. The Arabs had no idea what they were, but Taffy told them they were land mines. immediately the Arabs wanted to leave the **HAINULT** as they feared an explosion. Taffy assured them that the mines were not equipped with detonators and therefore safe, but from then onwards neither the Arabs nor the Greeks would venture on to the vessel

By now the cargo was impeding further pumping and there was still a large volume of water to remove. taffy decided that it was time to pump dry the engine-room, and the hoses were transferred down through the skylights to the floor of the engine-room. As the water level dropped the vessel began to rise. They continued to pump till the engine-room space was dry and the vessel began to swing. She could not swing very far as both her anchors were down. The windlass was damaged and corroded beyond repair thus preventing the anchors being raised in the conventional way. Steel cables were brought on board and passed through each of the hawse pipes and lowered down and shackled to the anchor chains. The capstans on the **HAINULT** were used to raise the anchor chains, and as the shackles appeared on deck the chains were chocked. Down went the cables again and were re-shackled and further anchor chain was brought on board.

Meanwhile Taffy had brought on board a flexible steam hose which he connected to one of the pumps. He had previously stripped down this pump, and although badly corroded on its exterior, he could find little wrong with is internal working parts. When it had been warmed through, he connected it to No.1 hold suction and from the side of the vessel dirty water started emerging. By late evening that hold was dry and he turned his attention to No.2 hold.

The ship breakers in Algiers decided that they were not interested in a vessel that was loaded with such a lethal cargo. Hassan was in constant contact with the Ministry of Libyan Affairs as to what to do with the vessel. The British Army was still in distinct evidence in Libya and came to the rescue. The vessel, the **HASSE** was towed round to Benghazi and tied up to the quay where hundreds of squaddies slowly unloaded the mines and transferred them to a fleet of army lorries. The lorries left the harbour and took the cargo out into the desert where a controlled explosion removed any hazard they might have caused. A Maltese company decided that they would buy the vessel and after the **HAINULT** had bunkered, set off with the **HASSE** in tow. She was to be towed to the same yard where they had, years before towed the PAPA D. The tow was uneventful and Hassan Kamel, in Bill Samuels opinion would make a good skipper and navigator but had to be hardened up a bit to make him suitable for salvage work.

On returning to Benghazi the work was well under way in raising the second half of a ship that had broken its back. The first half had been raised and had been patched up as soon as it floated and was now moored to a quay awaiting the raising of the second half. Within a week it was afloat and speedily patched up, and the **STELLA I** and the **HAINULT** started the long tow to Algiers with the two halves in tow. There remained one small vessel that was sitting on the bottom with only its mast showing above the water. When Duff dived down he found that it was in a terrible state and lay in several pieces. Obviously it had suffered a violent explosion. Duff decided that it would be better to cut it up into sections and then lift the bits up and place them in barges. Ray George and two of his engineers donned scuba suits and spent hours down there cutting up first the bridge and the masts at its base as well as such things as the anchor cable and mast stays in preparation for the return of the other two tugs.

A week or so later found the other two tugs back at Benghazi, and the lifting of the large metal chunks out of the depths started. In the meantime a newly formed ship breakers had set up business west of Alexandria. It was now beneficial to take the remains there, and save the long passage to Algiers. Weeks went past before all the metal chunks were finally removed and placed in barges and they were cleared for the passage to the breakers.

The next port that was to be cleared was Derna, another shallow draught harbour. Her lay three sunken barges and two small tugs, one, a craft tug and the other a small docking tug. Camels were used to raise the two tugs and it was found that when they were both in turn brought to the surface, that they had damage only to the upper works and that there was no apparent damage to the hulls. This made life easy as they were pumped dry by the **HAINULT** and one by one they gracefully floated. Both the tugs were lashed together, and the **HAINULT** started the tow to Alexandria, where the breakers decided that the craft tug would be broken up and the docking tug could be sold on for rebuilding. Before the **HAINULT** left the breakers to return to Derna, three more from the consortium were put on board, and to Taffy's dismay, one of them was the ex Chief Engineer from the **CERCUR**. Taffy could not tolerate the man and vowed that once they were back with the **STELLAs**, that the man would have to take up permanent residence on one of the other tugs. One of the others that Taffy did however take to, was an Egyptian named Abdul Kafir, who had previously sailed on the tug **AGILE** when she had been based in the Suez Canal. By the time they reached Derna, Taffy was convinced that he had found a worthy replacement.

Thank goodness they had brought the bucket grabs with them. The sunken barges were loaded with crates and some loose cargo. The diver took two days securing wires round some of the larger crates in the first barge before the **STELLAs** could start lifting out the cargo and placing in barges. Down went the grabs and a start was made on removing the loose cargo. Hours later it was found that each successive lift was only grabfulls of water. it was decided to try a new technique in lifting the barge directly from the bottom. Heavy towing wires were run down over the bows of both **STELLAs** and these were secured as best they could to the forward and aft sections of the sunken barge. Both **STELLAs** started hauling very slowly. The bows of both tugs started dipping alarmingly, so Duff and Derek Brown ordered the water in the fore peak tanks to be jettisoned. As the water spewed out of the tugs' sides the bows very slowly rose slightly and at last the barge started lifting from its watery grave. As soon as its hatches were above water the **HAINULT** put her hoses on board and started pumping. As the decks gradually cleared of water the two **STELLAs** removed their lifting cables and they too put their hoses on board. By nightfall the barge was dry and moored to the quay.

The second barge was raised in the same manner with no difficulties. The third was cleared and raised, but when pumping commenced the level of water in the barge lowered very slowly. The hose from the **STELLAs** were also put on board and although they lowered the water level considerably, it was obvious that the barge was badly holed. When the water level refused to drop any further, the two **STELLAs** unshipped their hoses and with the **HAINULT's** pumps still pumping, pushed the barge into the shallows till the **STELLAs** were grazing their bottoms. As the **HAINULT** pushed the barge still farther the **STELLA's** hoses snaked out of the barges hold and were brought back on board. When the barge grounded in about six feet of water and the **HAINULT** stopped her pumps.

Taffy could find no damage to the sides of the hull, but found a large hole in the bottom. Close inspection revealed that the bottom of the barge had corroded away in many places making it unsuitable for plating up. Later that day some of Taffy's men started cutting up the barge down to the waterline. As each part was cut up, it was lifted up by the **HAINULT's** derrick and brought out into deeper water where the **STELLAs** took over and ferried the chunks across the harbour and deposited them in the barges that had already been raised. The part that was left underwater had heavy lifting lugs welded to it, and the three tugs together dragged this section into deeper water, where the two **STELLAs** again lifted it to the surface. This time however it was lifted up on to the decks of the two barges and lashed to the decks. Very slowly the two barges were towed out of the harbour by the **STELLAs** towards Egypt for their last journey.

The **HAINULT** followed the small convoy as she was to attend to another small coaster that was wallowing in shallow water further along the coast. This was quite a modern vessel called the **NEDGMO**, a twin screwed diesel vessel, of some 800tons, that was sitting on the bottom in about ten feet of water. She looked in pristine condition and Bill Samuels inquired as to why the vessel had not been refloated before. he was told that the **NEDGMO** had run ashore when a patrol vessel had chased it, as it was suspected of drug trafficking. "It had just been left there", was the reply. On boarding it the hatches were found to be open, but she was devoid of cargo. Her two holds and engine-room all contained about six feet of water. Taffy felt sure that there were no holes in the vessel and that refloating would be simple, just pump her dry.

The following morning the hoses were hoisted on board and the pumps started. By noon there was movement of the vessel, and by late evening she was afloat. Pumping continued overnight till she was dry. In the morning light Taffy re-boarded her and found that there had been no ingress of water in any of the spaces. There was considerable fuel oil in her tanks and taffy reckoned that when the motors dried, that they would be able to get the engines started and that the vessel could make her own way to the nearest port which was still Derna.

Remembering Ray George's success on the **SANDY WATERS** with the steam cleaning, Taffy ran a steam hose from the **HAINULT** and steam cleaned the small dynamo and the three other electric motors in the engine-room. The steering gear motors were of the totally enclosed type. The next morning the dynamo which was driven by a small two cylinder engine was started, and started firing after only a couple of swings of the starting handle. The main engines were battery started, and, on inspection it was found that the batteries were well run down. Rather than wait for the batteries to be charged up, Taffy ran leads from the **HAINULT's** dynamos down to the starter motors and attempted to start one of the main engines. Although everything electrical on the **HAINULT** had been switched off, the **HAINULT's** generator slowed down a bit as the took the starting load. Gradually the starter motor began to warm up through continued attempts at starting, when suddenly the engine burst into life and ran smoothly. The leads were transferred to the other engine's starter motor, and immediately the engine started. Now they were running, the other equipment including the steering gear could be tested. It was found to be in good working order but a bit sluggish. The **HAINULT** escorted her to Derna where she was placed in the hands of the shipping agent.

Tobruk was the last harbour to be cleared, and they were indeed nearing the end of their contract. Duff, Taffy and Angel began to think about what they would do at the end of their contract. Duff and Taffy had amassed a fortune by anyone's standards, and they clearly wanted to continue living off the sea to end their days. Taffy suggested that they buy the **NEDGMO** and take her back to the UK and Angel agreed to stay with them.

First Tobruk harbour had to be cleared, but the agent in Derna was contacted so that a sale could be arranged. Immediately they were told that the vessel could be theirs at any fair price that they offered.. The Arabs asked for volunteers to stay on the **STELLAs** for a further two years. Bill Samuels and Derek Brown and a couple of the other officers and a few of the crewmen decided to work for the consortium. The conditions that were being offered were good:- six months on and three months off, with substantial terminal gratuity. Duff, Taffy ,Angel and Ray George and several others decided that it was time to go home when Tobruk was finally cleared.

Along the beach were a few barges that were patched up, and a coaster was raised. the British Army, still being in occupation were called upon to blow up many of the underwater obstructions and these were lifted to the surface in bits. This meant the divers spending long hours beneath the surface while they attached lifting cables to the bits of wreckage. It was a couple of months work before the harbour was clear. By this time the **NEDGMO** had been brought round to the harbour and tied up to the quay in front of King Idris's palace. Tobruk was the only deep water harbour on the Libyan coast, and as oil had recently been found it was envisaged that large tankers would eventually be docking there.

Duff and Taffy decided that half of the salvage money that they had received on the contract, they would share amongst the crew of the three tugs, as they were more than satisfied with the price of the sale of the tugs.

When all the salvage work was complete, it was a month short of the two years, and Duff felt that it would only be fair to the new owners that all three craft were dry-docked before they were handed over. Days later the three tugs set off for Alexandria where they were to dry-dock. On the way there they towed patched up barges and the coaster that had been raised. All three vessels were well down in the water as they had all been loaded with the debris that had been raised. Four days later the tugs emerged from the dry docks with their bottoms painted and their funnels painted a buff colour with black tops. Gone were the red funnels with the intermingled HTC. For many of them the trip back to Tobruk was a nostalgic one as many of them would be parting company. Duff was swift in making and finalising all the financial arrangements. All the terminal gratuities and salvage moneys were paid into the crew's accounts in the UK and it was time to start work on the **NEDGMO**.

There was not much in the way of accommodation on board the **NEDGMO** and this was going to be a problem to get everyone home. The weather at that time of year was far too hot for everyone to stay on deck for the whole of the day, and to stay in the holds would be unbearable. The deck could be rigged with awnings, but if they met a strong wind on the way home the shelter would be of little benefit. In the end it was decided for comfort's sake that half of those returning to the UK would go by land. Duff decided that they would all make the trip to Italy to drop off those who were going to travel overland and then return to Tobruk for a thorough inspection of the vessel before they made the trip home. The awnings were rigged on the **NEDGMO** for this short trip and they set off for Naples. Two days later found the **NEDGMO** passing through the Straits of Messina and into cooler climes before entering Naples. The home-going crew disembarked and their gear was brought up from the hold. The return to Tobruk was uneventful, and they were disappointed to find neither the **HAINULT** nor the **STELLAs** there.

Taffy and the engineers gave the engines and the auxiliaries a good overhaul and they bunkered and provisioned up in preparation of sailing.

Leaving Tobruk in the blazing heat they rounded the headland and turned west, passing the scenes of their salvages on the way. When they were nearing the coat of Tunisia, they met a familiar sight. There on apparently on a parallel course was the **HAINULT**. As they drew closer they found that she was unmanned and drifting. Her lifeboats were gone but the vessel showed no signs of disarray. Flashy quickly radioed the agent in Benghazi inquiring about the welfare of the **HAINULT**, only to be told that she had been abandoned by her crew two days earlier. The crew had apparently landed and were all safe.

Moving alongside they tied up to her and climbed on board. The boilers were of course stone cold and the levels of water were also very low. Taffy examined all the other tanks and found that they were as dry as a bone. There were no facilities on the **NEDGMO** to pump oil or water out of the **NEDGMO** , and the bilge pump could not be connected to either, but Taffy knew what gear there was in the **HAINULT's** hold. He knew that there were some small volume pumps that could be used to transfer both oil and a small quantity of water to at least get the engines going. The derrick on the **NEDGMO** was rigged and raised and swung over the **HAINULT's** hold and very slowly the pumps were raised out of the hold and placed on the deck of the **NEDGMO**. These were diesel driven and very quickly they were started and the life-giving liquids were transferred from one vessel to the other.

With ropes fastening them side by side, the two made for the port of Tunis. By the time Tunis was in sight, Taffy had all the oil transferred to the high level tanks and the furnaces on one boiler were flashed up. The burners being gravity fed for this part of the exercise were not working efficiently and thick volumes of smoke were emerging from the funnel. By the time they entered Tunis the boiler had reached a pressure of 30lbs/sq.inch, and Taffy had been able to get the forced draught fans going, and in doing so, the intensity of the smoke had died down to a thin whisper. Three hours later a bunkering tanker came alongside and filled her tanks and topped up those of the **NEDGMO**.

The agent in Benghazi was telephoned and was asked for a direct line to the owners of the consortium. The agent was unable to arrange this as it seemed that the consortium had faded into oblivion.

To take the **HAINULT** home would not be difficult as they had plenty of men to man both vessels.

The **HAINULT** and the **NEDGMO** sailed out of Tunis for to Tangiers where they would re-bunker for the final leg to the UK. Once againon this leg they spotted the **CHEYNEY** still tied up in exactly the same spot as she had been on their previous visits. Leaving Tangiers, Taffy and some of the engineers opened up some of the auxiliaries that were not in use and found that she had been well looked after. Why was it that the **HAINULT** had been abandoned? After all she had only run out of fuel. Why had the radio operator not radioed for a vessel to come out to her and re-fuel her? Why was it that she had not radioed for help and been towed back into port? These were the questions that were never answered.

The trip to the UK was uneventful and both vessels tied up by the yard at Blackwall that they all knew so well. Taffy and Duff were beginning to tire of the raw life that they had been leading for so many years. They were both nearing fifty and both felt that they should start taking life a bit easy as they were both men of considerable wealth.

First they approached the courts about the ownership of the **HAINULT**. For the next six months the various authorities tried to trace the consortium without success. It appeared that they had disappeared from the face of the earth. The **STELLAs** were still going about their business but were crewed by Egyptians who operated through agents. In the end the courts decided that HTC had salvaged the **HAINULT** and therefore were the rightful owners.

Over the next four months the **NEDGMO** was converted to a pleasure cruiser, and after much negotiation ran a daily service from Westminster Pier to France, and Angel did all the catering.

Taffy bought the yard at Blackwall, and the **HAINULT** was brought into one of the dry-docks after she was repainted in her original colours and she became a museum-piece. On the side of the dry-dock Taffy had a small brick-built museum erected and inside was a write-up of all the salvage operations carried out by the **HAINULT** both during and after the war. The walls were adorned with many of the photos of the operations.

Long live the **HAINULT 4367**